The Savage Hills

Center Point
Large Print

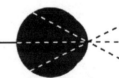

**This Large Print Book carries the
Seal of Approval of N.A.V.H.**

The Savage Hills

D. B. NEWTON

CENTER POINT LARGE PRINT
THORNDIKE, MAINE

ISBN: 978-1-62899-978-5 (hardcover)
ISBN: 978-1-62899-982-2 (paperback)

Library of Congress Cataloging-in-Publication Data

Names: Newton, D. B. (Dwight Bennett), 1916– author.
Title: The savage hills / D. B. Newton.
Description: Center Point Large Print edition. | Thorndike, Maine :
Center Point Large Print, 2016. | ©1964
Identifiers: LCCN 2016008256| ISBN 9781628999785
    (hardcover : alk. paper) | ISBN 9781628999822 (pbk. : alk. paper)
Subjects: LCSH: Large type books. | GSAFD: Western stories.
Classification: LCC PS3527.E91767 S28 1994 | DDC 813/.52—dc23
LC record available at http://lccn.loc.gov/2016008256

The Savage Hills

CHAPTER I

The piebald was an ugly, knotheaded brute that didn't want to be ridden, but the fellow up top was taking no foolishness from him. He had a coiled rope and at every pitch he slammed it against the hard skull, did it again and again until the horse laid back its ears and squealed with fury. Jim Bannister, who had been a mustanger himself, knew a superb job of riding when he saw one; reining in to watch, he could feel his own teeth aching to the lunge of those braced forelegs that fairly made the dust-streaked air tremble. Yet he could tell that the horse was already beaten, and fast losing steam.

He spoke to his sorrel now and rode slowly forward as the piebald came to a stand, trembling and snorting and dripping sweat into the dust. Bannister pushed his hat back with a thumbnail. "Nice going," he observed.

The rider, apparently unaware till now of an audience, snapped his head around sharply. Intent black eyes peered at him. They looked old, and so did the mouth, tightlipped between deep, bracketing lines; still, Bannister could see that the face was young—very young, in fact. He was really only a kid, not yet eighteen, in all likelihood. He wore jeans that were out at one knee, and frayed along the pockets. His shirt was faded, colorless; the boot he lifted across the piebald's shoulder while lighting down was badly scuffed and worn at the heel. Not troubling to answer the stranger's comment, he began stripping off the saddle.

Jim Bannister indicated the corral where there were a dozen or so other horses, all about a match for the piebald. "These broncs belong to you?"

The youngster looked at him again, shoved lank black hair back from his forehead. "These bangtails?" he said, with a touch of scorn. "Naw. They're old man Murdock's. He picked 'em up cheap, off some Indian, and he's payin' me to knock the rough edges off. Thinks he's got a buyer over to Cabra Springs."

"They worth anything?"

"For glue, maybe. Ain't nothin' but range scrubs. Only a skinflint like Murdock would waste time on 'em."

This jibed with Bannister's own estimate, now that he had had a closer look. "No, they don't look like much."

"They can fight like hell, just the same! I'm glad that was the last of 'em!"

The young fellow dragged his saddle free and let it drop into the dust, using the spare and studied movements of one whose body had been pounded stiff and sore. The piebald didn't want to go back into the pen; the boy was trying to drag it in by

8

main force when Jim Bannister quickly kneed the sorrel over, swung his hat in the brute's face and sent him skittering across the lowered bar. The youngster, breathing hard, threw Jim a brief look of thanks and went in after the horse to retrieve his bridle. When he climbed out of the corral and set the poles in place again, he appeared close to exhaustion, moving almost like someone in a stupor.

He looked around, located a shapeless hat where it lay trampled in the dust, picked it up and beat it against his knee. Pulling it on, he said, "Nothing left to do now, I guess, but go collect what I got coming." He hung the bridle over one shoulder and leaned down for the battered saddle. Its weight pulled him into a slantwise stride as he walked away across the clearing in the jackpine.

This place was obviously a species of trail-side trading post, built to deal with the scattered ranches and the occasional traveler through these parts. It was likely doing well enough. The store itself, a good-sized log building, had a shake roof and a gallery, and a storage room tacked on at the rear. There were a horse shed and other smaller buildings, scattered around haphazardly. There was the pole corral, with the dozen head of range scrubs in it, and a parked wagon that the trader must use for hauling supplies. A spring had been rocked in to form a pool, the runoff making a stream that meandered across the clearing; here, a couple of planks served for a bridge.

The kid crossed the bridge and walked over to the horse shed, leaving his saddle on the ground while he opened the door to what appeared to be a tack room. When he came out, carrying a skimpy-looking blanket roll, Jim Bannister was helping himself to a drink at the spring while the sorrel muzzled the water of the runoff. The boy dropped the blankets by his saddle, then came over and took the dipper Bannister handed him. He flipped out the last drops, filled it again and drank.

Bannister said, "I don't know this country. You mentioned something called Cabra Springs. Would that be the nearest town?"

"Naw—it's only a shipping point on the railroad." The kid gestured vaguely eastward with the dipper. "Nearest town is Downey, the county seat. Maybe ten miles south by the wagon road."

Bannister, who had ridden in from the west, now knew three compass points to avoid. "What's that way?" he asked, indicating the pile-up of timbered ridges that marched northward, always climbing. The youngster looked, considering it for a moment; but he shook his head.

"Couldn't tell you. Seems I heard there's a pass, then some more up-and-down country like this, with some cattle outfits. But you better ask old Murdock. I don't know the country either." He bent and splashed spring water over his face and head, cutting the dust.

"I thought your folks might live around here."

"My folks?" The young fellow peered at him through the fingers he had spread to comb back dripping black hair. It was, somehow, a look of such eloquence Jim Bannister knew he would never forget it. But when the boy answered, his voice was completely matter of fact and without a trace of self-pity. "I got no folks."

He palmed water from his cheeks, pulled on the shapeless wad of felt he called a hat, and went on to the main building that housed the store. Jim Bannister watched him cross the porch, not certain what it was about the boy that intrigued him unless it was that air of defiant independence—the manner, unusual in one so young, of having survived rough going without asking quarter of anyone.

Bannister paused for a moment to lean and examine the sorrel's right foreleg, running big, trained hands over the hard muscle. Afterward, straightening, he stood with one hand on the sorrel's neck while he studied the warm stillness, concentrating especially on the stretch of country he had just traveled. He was a big man, this Jim Bannister, bigger than most—a yellow-haired giant of a fellow, with the trailstained clothing of one constantly on the move; his pale eyes held a thoughtful, ingrained wariness.

As the boy had named it, this was indeed up-and-down country—rock-ribbed, range-and-timber country. It was remote and little traveled, which suited Jim Bannister's purpose; but a man in his position would do well to learn as much as he could about it, rather than trying to ride it blind. Accordingly, though a shade reluctant, he led the sorrel over to the log store building; there he hung the reins over a porch rail that still bore patches of rough bark, and walked inside.

The interior was about what he would have expected—crudely built, poorly lit, overcrowded with merchandise. Everything imaginable that a hill-country rancher might be induced to buy here, rather than ride the extra miles to town, could probably be found among the stuff that filled the wooden bins, overflowed the counters, and dangled from wall pegs.

A sound of quarreling voices greeted Bannister as he paused on the threshold; he looked and saw the black-haired horsebreaker glaring, tense with fury, at an old man who leaned toward him across a counter with both hands pressed flat upon its top.

"I don't know what you're talking about," the boy was saying stoutly. "I did my job and now I want my money—like you promised."

"And I'm telling you, I'll pay after you and Harry Jones deliver those broncs at railhead."

"Oh, no, Mr. Murdock—you're wrong! There

was nothing in our deal about me helping deliver. We agreed I was to get two fifty a head, thre rides each to take the starch out. I'm willing enough to trail along to Cabra Springs, if you want me to—but I'll have to ask extra pay."

"Why, you young pup! Are you trying to dictate terms to me?" Murdock came to his full height. He had a mean eye and a mouth like a trap. His unhealthy, yellowish skin was furred below the gaunted cheeks with a patchy beard stubble of black and gray and white—nearly the same colors as the piebald in the corral. What hair he had left lay thinly across his scalp. His neck was like a turkey gobbler's, inside the candy-striped shirt he wore buttoned at the throat without a collar.

"You'll take whatever I say you're worth, Evans!" he snapped. He reached down to open a cash drawer below the counter; coins clinked and paper money rustled under his searching fingers. "As for making delivery—you can forget about that. I want no more dealings with the likes of you. . . . Here!" He pushed the drawer closed, tossed a coin on the wood in front of the boy. Bannister saw the dull gleam of gold—a double eagle. "Take this and get out!"

The Evans kid merely looked at the money, without touching it. He said, "That's only twenty dollars. It's thirty you owe me."

Old Murdock shoved a bony forefinger under the kid's nose; plainly he thought he could get away with anything, so long as he backed it up with bluster. "You took near a week with those horses—eating my grub while you did it, feeding my oats to that crowbait roan of yours. Maybe you figured I wouldn't deduct for it."

"Ten dollars' worth?" The youngster looked as though he'd been slapped. His whole body went stiff, and when he spoke again he had trouble keeping his voice under control. For all his toughness, he gave Bannister the impression of fighting back a sob of frustration. "You damned skinflint! Maybe we'll see what the sheriff has to say!"

"Suits me!" The old man bobbed his gaunt head. "Sure, you just go tell Sid Parrott I agreed to give thirty dollars to some out-of-pockets drifter kid, and see how much of that he believes!" He set a forefinger on the gold coin, shoved it firmly across the counter. "This is probably more than you ever had in your pocket at one time in your life. It's every red cent you'll get out of me!"

The tall man in the doorway said quietly, "Pay him the other ten, Murdock."

"Who says?" The man's glance jerked around. His eyes narrowed in quick hostility. "You stay out of this—whoever you are!"

"Looks like *somebody* better get in it," Bannister said, walking forward. "I've gentled some horses in my time. I figure the kid's asking a fair price—and a deal's a deal."

14

His calm insistence seemed to set Murdock back a little. But the old man still had plenty of argument left in him. "How about the piebald? He's as wild as the day I bought him—I seen you two through the window, fighting him into the corral."

"The piebald's an outlaw," young Evans told him flatly. "Nobody'll ever do much with him. But the rest all took to gentlin' real good. I done a job for you, Murdock. I swear I did!"

Murdock sneered openly in disbelief. Jim Bannister's lips felt stiff with anger as he repeated crisply, "Pay him!"

This time the old man's attention was brought fully on the tall stranger; his yellow-lidded stare narrowed, the sharp black eyes crawling with thought. They mirrored a decision, and for a moment Bannister actually thought the old man was knuckling under to pressure.

For Murdock reached a hand below the counter again as though to open the cash drawer. But instead his hand found a big hogleg revolver and came up holding it. The thing was done so deliberately that, for once in his life, Bannister was taken by surprise.

"Lift 'em, mister!" the old man snapped. "Don't touch your holster!"

Chagrin was a sour emotion in Bannister, but as yet he felt no real alarm. More curious than anything else, he slowly lifted his hands to shoulder height. Murdock rested his wrist on the edge of the counter, steadying the weight of the weapon he held. Without turning his head he sent a shout toward a closed door that, Bannister judged, must lead to the storeroom. "Harry! Come in here. Make it quick!"

When there was no immediate response he called again, louder. A moment later the door opened. The man who hurried in was rail lean, of an indefinite age, with a slight cast in one eye and shoulders rounded by heavy labor. He laid a hammer on the counter and stripped off a pair of heavy gloves, waiting for orders. Murdock nodded curtly toward Jim Bannister.

"His gun. Get it."

Bannister felt the muscles across his shoulders and belly go suddenly tight. "Hold on, now! Don't make any mistake!" he said sharply.

"Don't *you!*" the old man retorted, and the hogleg's muzzle centered more definitely on the middle of the blond stranger's chest.

The handyman, Harry Jones, was circling the counter, coming up behind Bannister. The latter flicked a look at Young Evans and saw him scowling, puzzled at this turn of events. Then an arm roped with stringy muscle snaked into the edge of Bannister's vision and he felt his holster lose its weight. Harry stepped back, moving away again toward the counter. Murdock nodded approval.

"Just keep him covered while I do a little checking. But watch him close. If I'm guessing right, he could be dangerous!"

Harry Jones took a two-fisted grip on the weapon. Seeing the wild edge to his look, Bannister's breathing went shallow; a scared amateur, with a gun in his hands, was twice as dangerous as any professional killer. Meanwhile, Murdock had laid his own gun aside and, from somewhere under the counter, brought out a considerable stack of what Bannister recognized instantly to be reward dodgers.

"I make a collection of these," he said briefly. "Keeping a place here on the back trails, a man never knows who might come along. And it's paid off, a time or two." He wet a splayed thumb on his tongue and began riffling through the stiff sheets of paper with practiced swiftness. Bannister watched in growing apprehension. A glance at the Evans kid showed him looking on with an expression of blank puzzlement.

Almost at once old Murdock gave a grunt of satisfaction, pulled one poster out of the stack and shoved the rest aside. "I knew I remembered!" He looked from the block of printing to the prisoner, and nodded. "Description fits; size, everything!"

"Probably fits a thousand other men, too," Bannister said in chill anger.

But the old fellow was unperturbed. "Not many

17

come *that* big. And not many carry that big a price, either!" Greed made his hand tremble as he ran it across his sunken cheeks; he picked up the hogleg revolver again. "I'll take him now, Harry. You saddle a horse. Scoot down to town and find the sheriff. Tell him I'm holding Jim Bannister here—with twelve thousand in syndicate money on his head!"

CHAPTER II

Bannister quelled the sharp rise of alarm that bothered his breathing. "This is damned foolishness!" he snapped. "You think I'm going to stand around waiting while you get a sheriff up here? Just because you've mixed me up with somebody on a stupid reward dodger?"

"Why not? I got nothing to lose if I'm wrong," Murdock pointed out complacently. "And everything to gain if I'm right. Yeah, I think you'll wait!" He threw a look at his helper. "I told you to get started."

Harry Jones nodded; mumbling something. He laid the captured sixgun on the counter and went hurrying out through the back of the store, whipping off his apron as he went. Murdock stepped to close the storeroom door, saying as he did so, "What tipped me off was the thing you said about having worked with horses. I remembered then that Jim Bannister was a horse rancher down in New Mexico, before he got into that trouble with Western Development and killed their man for them. It started me thinking."

To go on denying the truth was a waste of effort. Bannister said coldly, "Do I have to keep my hands in the air?"

"No, that's all right, Bannister—you can put 'em

19

down." Murdock waved the gun barrel. "There's a crate behind you. Have a seat. We might as well be easy." He rounded the end of the counter, carefully straddled a nail keg and leaned his shoulders against the wood. Outside, there was a sudden noise of a horse departing; Bannister, turning, saw Harry Jones go flashing past the open door, astride a bony-looking gray. The sound of galloping hoofs quickly thinned and faded.

"I said, have a seat," Murdock repeated, and Bannister shrugged as he complied. "I'm right curious," the storekeeper went on pleasantly, "to know how any man can be worth twelve thousand to the syndicate. Must have been a pretty important kingpin you salivated." His eyes narrowed shrewdly. "Or do they just want to set an example for other people who don't happen to like the outfit? Show 'em nobody can murder a Western Development agent and get away with it? I never knew one of them Eastern syndicates that was what you called popular."

Bannister wasn't even listening. He had suddenly seen what the Evans kid was up to.

Unobserved by Murdock, who sat with his back against the counter with the heavy sixshooter resting on one thigh, the youngster was staring as though in fascination at that other revolver—the one Harry Jones had taken from the prisoner and left lying on the wood. The gleam of gunmetal seemed to act on him like a magnet. Bannister saw him lift a boot, move it cautiously forward and set it down again without sound. His hand began to reach. His eyes had a kind of desperate intensity.

In the light of what was to happen next, Bannister could wish he had shouted at the kid and ordered him to stand away. But just at the moment it seemed to be his job to keep the old man talking, keep him unconscious of the thing happening behind him. He found his voice; it sounded too loud as he spoke the first thought that entered his head: "*You* seem to like the syndicates well enough—at least, you don't mind turning their enemies over for them to hang!"

The old man positively smirked. "For twelve thousand? Know anyone that wouldn't?"

It was from a depth of bitter experience that Bannister answered heavily, "Damned few! Precious damn few, at that!"

And then the boy made his play. He took the remaining distance in a single stride, grabbing for the sixshooter—and in his anxiety, over-reached. His fingers struck the barrel, set the thing spinning. Helpless to do more than watch, Bannister saw the boy's face go deathly pale as he fought to seize the weapon and prevent it from dropping out of reach on the far side of the counter.

Old Murdock had already taken warning and was twisted about on his keg, his mouth gaping.

He seemed belatedly to remember the gun in his own hand, and brought the barrel swinging around just as the kid managed to get his fingers on the elusive sixshooter. Young Evans shouted at him hoarsely: "No! Don't!"

Murdock fired.

He was too hasty and he missed widely. But the boy didn't. Half sprawled against the counter, he reacted to the blast of muzzle flame by yanking the trigger, with an unthinking convulsion of his whole body. His bullet took Murdock squarely in the chest and knocked the old man backward, his nail keg overturning under him. Murdock fell, all in a tangle of flung arms and legs, with a look of the most utter incredulity stamped upon his face.

It was over and done, as quickly as that. With the concussion of mingled gunshots still throbbing in his head, Bannister got his legs under him. He strode forward, gave the keg a boot so that it rolled ponderously out of the way; he stood a moment looking at the blood on Murdock's chest and at the wide and staring eyes. He turned then and nodded to the boy. "You fixed him," he said bluntly. "You fixed him good!"

"You mean he's *dead?*" The boy's eyes were black holes in a face drained of color. "He shouldn't of—I never meant—"

"Maybe you never meant, but you sure as hell *did!*" Though there could hardly be any doubt,

Bannister knelt for a closer look. As he did something started to churn inside him; his throat clogged on a rising obstruction and he had to swallow, hard. He had never learned to look on death with indifference—not the kind of bloody wreckage the bullet, at these close quarters, had made of this man.

So he turned away his eyes—and saw the hog-leg revolver lying where it had fallen from the dead man's fingers. He was moving to pick it up when he heard the boy's quick exclamation: "No you don't!" He lifted his head, found the muzzle of his own gun trained squarely on him.

"Don't touch it!"

"*Now* what's got into you?" Bannister demanded, scowling, but something stayed his hand.

The young fellow said, in the same hard voice, "Stand up!" And after Bannister had done so, moving slowly: "Now give it a kick!"

Face expressionless, Bannister nudged the gun with a boot and sent it scooting over the tough floorboards to strike the wall. "Go easy, kid!" he said gruffly. "Don't lose your head! I know you were only trying to give me a chance to make a break. You and I are on the same side in this!"

"I'm on nobody's side!" the boy retorted. "And now that I've killed a man, I guess I can always do it again—so don't crowd me!"

He searched the room, almost as though looking for hidden enemies, and thus his glance lit upon the double eagle that still lay on the counter where Murdock had placed it. He picked it up in his free hand and fingered it, and Bannister could see the idea building behind his eyes. Their expression settled into a crafty keenness; abruptly he shoved the gold coin into his pocket and was on his way around the end of the counter. He found the cash drawer, yanked it open and stood for a moment staring hungrily at what he saw inside. He thrust a hand in, brought it out gripping a wad of crumpled bills.

Jim Bannister said coldly, "I'd put that back, kid. All but ten dollars—that's how much he still owed you."

The youngster's angry stare whipped at him; his mouth tightened in defiance. "The hell with what you'd do!"

"All right." Bannister shrugged. "Maybe he forced you to shoot him. It gives you no excuse to turn thief. That's your own doing!"

His words got him a glare of rage. The young fellow's hand clutched the money defiantly and, in the stillness, Jim Bannister could hear the harsh rasp of the boy's breathing. So complete was the stillness, there with the body of the dead man lying between them, that the unexpected sound of a ridden horse seemed to break startlingly loud across the sunlit world outside.

The youngster's head jerked in alarm; and a step carried Bannister to the window where, through dusty glass, he saw a rider moving out of the timber. "Somebody coming?" the boy demanded hoarsely.

Bannister gave a grunt. "It's Harry Jones. Must not have been out of hearing yet—at least, he seems to have heard those gunshots. . . ."

The boy stood motionless in an agony of indecision, while the mutter of hoofsounds swelled. Suddenly, with a grimace, he plucked a single bill from the wad and flung the rest back into the drawer. Bannister nodded in approval. "Now you're using your head," he commented; but young Evans didn't even seem to hear. Pocketing his ten dollars, he came around from behind the counter and his boots pounded the floorboards as he crossed the room to the open door. On the gallery outside he halted, legs spread and Bannister's gun in his hand. Harry Jones was still scarcely in pistol range when the boy whipped up the revolver and threw off a hurried bullet.

The kick of the gun flung the boy's arm head high; he pulled it down and fired again, echoes of the two shots bouncing and threading away across the slopes and timbered ridges. Bannister, through the window, saw the rider pull in so sharply that his horse reared and all but spilled him off the saddle. While the gray danced nervously under him, Harry Jones craned to peer at the figure on the shadowed porch. One look was enough. Next moment he had pulled the animal around and was gone again, abruptly melting back into the safety of the timber; the dust he had lifted hung golden-yellow in the air behind him.

But his appearance must have triggered panic in the Evans youngster, for already the boy was in motion, vaulting the porch rail to hurl himself at Jim Bannister's sorrel. He tore the reins loose, got a stirrup and was reaching for the pommel before he seemed to remember his right hand still had a gun in it. He stuffed the weapon clumsily behind his waist belt and was just hauling astride when Bannister came hurrying out onto the store verandah.

"Kid!" Bannister shouted at him. "What are you up to? Wait, damn it!"

The boy flung him a single, frantic look; then he was kicking the sorrel's flanks with both bootheels and the horse was leaping forward under him. Bannister's second shout went totally unheard; he hauled up, one hand against a roof prop, and scowled as he saw his sorrel disappearing in the direction of the hills to the northward—his horse, his gun and saddle, and every other thing he owned. In a matter of moments the pound of shod hoofs was quickly swallowed by the crowding timber, as though by a blotter.

Jim Bannister moved his shoulders angrily,

and swore. Having vented his feelings, he looked again to the south where Harry Jones had vanished. The tawny dust there had long since thinned and settled. The shots had scared the fellow off and this time, Jim Bannister was willing to wager, he wouldn't be coming back until he found a lawman. Forgetting any danger from that source, at least for the time being, he turned and walked back into the building.

His first thought was a covering for the body of the dead man, this partly from consideration for the dead but also because the sight of the staring eyes made him feel queasy in the region of his stomach. He found a pile of cheap blankets on the counter, shook one out and spread it over old Murdock's bloody remains, and then felt somewhat better. Next he went and picked Murdock's hogleg revolver up off the floor. The old man wouldn't be using it any longer, and it loaded the same caliber cartridges as the ones in his own belt. He replaced the empty shell and shoved the weapon into his holster and, with that important item taken care of, set about his further business.

The store carried a small stock of groceries, canned goods mostly. Bannister got himself a gunnysack and chose sparingly—beans and peaches and tomatoes, coffee and salt and sugar—estimating the price and scrupulously counting it out of the small amount of cash in his pocket. He added a few dollars to cover what he judged the gun was worth; in placing his money on the counter, he noticed the reward poster again and his expression turned bleak as he picked it up and glanced over the glaring block of print.

He had seen these things all too often before; every word he read was already emblazoned on his memory. He started to toss the poster aside, changed his mind and instead shoved it into a pocket. Taking his purchases, he walked out of the store, carefully closing the door after him.

There were a couple of horses in the shed, one of them an ugly, tough-jawed roan gelding. It wasn't much of a horse—not a great deal better than the scrubs in the corral. "Maybe he calls you a decent trade," Jim Bannister said bleakly, thinking of the sorrel and his other lost possessions, "but I'll damn well give him an argument!" He got the bridle from the sorry pile of stuff young Evans had left, and with some trouble induced the roan to accept the bit; leading it outside, he piled on blanket and saddle, and strapped the rest of the kid's meager belongings behind the cantle. He let out the stirrups to fit his long legs and swung astride.

From a rise north of the clearing he hauled in briefly for a final look back. Utter stillness lay over this upland. South, the Downey trail stretched, empty of travel. So far, at least, he supposed, so good.

The prints of the sorrel, spaced in the pattern of the Evans kid's hasty flight, showed in the trail that stretched north ahead of him. Jim Bannister raised his head toward the lift of the tangled hills and his mouth drew down sourly. He told the roan, "Let's get after that damned young fool before he runs my bronc into the ground!"

CHAPTER III

The roan didn't like a strange rider. It fought the bit, but Bannister settled it with a firm hand and used the spurs, and that straightened it out. In a moment they were climbing and the forest closed about them.

The way rose steadily—building, he supposed, toward that pass the Evans kid had mentioned, and which he hadn't had a chance to ask old Murdock about. The trail looped and climbed to accommodate itself to the rugged country. It was no country for pushing a horse, and he was at east pleased to note that the young fellow appeared to have given up his first hot flight.

The roan fell into an easy gait and Bannister held him at it, while a single white cloud swam high above the pine-topped ridges and the straight trunks laid their bands of shadow across him.

It was perhaps a half hour later, in a stand of aspen swamp flanking the trail, that he caught sight of the sorrel. The Evans kid probably thought he had it hidden, but Bannister's probing eyes found it—standing motionless amid the busy flickering of leaves. He started to draw rein, kept his pace instead and followed the narrow track down over a hump of rock. The slim-bodied trees were all around him then. Suddenly a figure stepped into the trail and sunlight glinted from a leveled gun barrel. He beard the boy saying, "All right. Pull up, and keep your hands in sight unless you want—"

The challenge died unfinished. The kid recognized him, with such ludicrous surprise as to put a grin of wry amusement on Jim Bannister. "It's you!"

"Who'd you think it was? The sheriff?"

The boy's face became splotched with the red stains of anger and embarrassment. "Well, it could have been," he said defensively. "Harry Jones might not have had to go clear to town." He added, "And, anyway, what's the idea of following me?"

"If you really want to know, I came to bring you your horse and your outfit—and get mine that you made off with!"

The kid hadn't even noticed it was his own horse and saddle Bannister was riding. He looked at them now, and the other saw him blink. He stammered and finally managed, "Guess I'm in luck that you did. That sorrel went lame."

"I'd have told you as much," Bannister replied, swinging down, "if you'd given me half a chance. I tried to yell, but you were in so damned much of a hurry!"

The kid had the decency to be ashamed of himself. His eyes wavered and he wet his lips. "Guess maybe I lost my head," he admitted. "But I'd never killed a man before. . . ."

"I just hope you haven't gone and crippled my horse for me."

Bannister slapped the roan's leathers into its owner's hand and, turning his back on him, pushed through the brush to where the sorrel stood half hidden among the trees.

The horse had had a bad time. Plastered with sweat and dust, it had to make an effort to raise its drooping head and swing it toward Bannister in greeting. He patted the lathered neck, then leaned to examine the near foreleg, carefully running his big, competent hands over it to test the muscle. Lifting the hoof from the ground, he flexed the action of knee joint and pastern; the animal submitted, though it bobbed its head in protest, and nudged his shoulder. Straightening, finally, he took the reins and led it, limping badly, back to the trail where the kid stood—sobered and a little shamefaced, he thought. There Bannister walked the animal up and down, critically observing.

"We took a spill earlier today," he explained briefly, "in some loose shale up near timberline. He started to limp maybe an hour afterward. That's the reason I was interested in those scrubs I saw you working on at Murdock's; thought at first I might try to make a trade, but at a closer look I knew it wasn't worth it. Even with a sore leg, the sorrel's a better animal—if he hasn't gone permanently lame."

The boy scowled. "What do you think?"

"Hard to say yet. Maybe I can by morning. At any rate, he's traveled as much as he's going to today."

"I'm—sorry," the young fellow muttered gruffly. "He's a good piece of horse."

"As good as they come," Jim Bannister agreed in a curt tone. He looked at the other, then, and saw the gun still in the boy's hand, forgotten.

"That belongs to me, too," he said. "I'll take it." He simply picked it out of the other's fingers, before the kid could do more than mouth a quick protest: "Hey, damn it!"

Deliberately, Bannister placed the gun in his holster, transferring Murdock's old hogleg to the waistband of his jeans. "And now," he said, "looks like that roan of yours will have to carry double."

The youngster made a quick protest, eying Bannister's big frame. "Not the both of us! It's too big a load."

"Can't be helped: Anyhow, it's only till we scare up a good place to make camp."

"This early?"

Bannister slanted a look at the sun, low above the ridges that cut the sky to the west of them. "It will be dark soon enough. If you want to keep pushing, that's your business; but it happens that I've got all the grub."

The youngster stabbed him with a look. "Do you always win every argument?" he said sourly. Not bothering to answer, Bannister turned again to the roan and swung into the saddle. He vacated a stirrup for the boy, grabbed an arm and hauled him up. He got the sorrel's reins and handed them back for the young fellow to lead; they rode on that way, accommodating their gait to the limping horse.

The site Jim Bannister picked for his camp was in a protected glen of rocks, well above the trail and hidden by timber; there was a grassy pocket handy within a hundred yards of it, for the horses, and a mossy seep spring. Bannister spent the last hour of daylight with the sorrel, working on that strained muscle. He concluded hopefully that morning should see an improvement. The last winy light drained out of the day, leaving the sky a steely white above the sharply outlined sawtooth pattern of timbered ridges, and he walked back to the campsite carrying an armload of down timber for the fire.

It seemed safe enough to have one; their camp was well protected and some distance from the pass road. Besides, they needed a fire—at such an altitude, nights could get chilly even at that season of the year. Dumping his load of wood, Bannister said, "I thought you'd have something cooking by this time."

The kid had been plowing through the gunny-sack; he settled back on his heels now, cans and bags of food strewn about him and a sullen look on his face. "I could have done a lot better than this, with Sam Murdock's whole stock to help myself from!"

"I admit it cramps a man's style," Bannister said coldly, "when he figures he should pay for what he takes." He saw the other's expression and added, "So what are you sneering about? Weren't you the one who put back that money?"

The youngster colored slightly. "Taking money is different. That's stealing."

"I don't see the difference."

"Hell! What's a few canned goods to anybody? Especially with the old man dead—who'd miss 'em?"

"I was thinking of his survivors."

"Hadn't none, that I know about." But then the boy frowned, remembering. "Well, come to think of it, I guess Harry Jones did mention an old maid sister. Lives down to Ouray or some such place."

"Then we'll say I paid *her* for this stuff."

Bannister shook out a handful of coffee beans from the sack and hammered them on a flat stone, using the butt of his sixgun. There was a battered coffeepot and other such utensils in his pack, and cold, clear water from the spring. By the time their meal was ready the last daylight was gone. As they ate, firelight washed the rocks that rose about them. Overhead the mountain stars were small explosions in the blue-black sky; later there would be a moon.

Bannister said, "Occurs to me I never did hear the first half of your name."

The young fellow looked at him over the lip of the coffeepot, from which they had been taking turns drinking. He seemed to debate whether to answer, then shrugged and said, "It's Clay. Clay Evans."

"All right, Clay Evans. Since we're going to be stuck with each other—for the next few hours, at any rate—maybe we should try to get along."

The boy set the pot back on the coals and sleeved his mouth. "If you mean it, how about lettin' me have that hogleg of Murdock's that's in your pack? It ain't much of a gun, and you got another."

Bannister considered him coldly. "You're pretty young to have already killed your first man," he pointed out. "Don't you think it would be a good idea if you let it end there?"

"If I'd just had a gun," young Evans retorted, "he wouldn't a dared push me around! It's always like that. All they have to do is figure a fellow can't force 'em to stick to a bargain. Especially if he has the look of a kid, without any friends to speak of."

That wasn't an easy argument to answer, because there was a lot of truth in it. Yet it bothered Jim Bannister, for it put him in mind of another young fellow, not many years older than this one, who was making something of a reputation for himself

36

down in Bannister's own home territory of New Mexico—fellow by the name of Will Bonney, who carried the difference on his hip and was embroiled deep in that sordid range squabble around Lincoln County. Bannister had never seen the man—this Billy the Kid, as they called him—but he had an uneasy feeling that he was sitting across the fire from another youngster with the potential for developing the same way.

After all, Clay Evans had made a good long step: He had notched his first kill. Or at least he *said* it was his first. . . .

Bannister studied the smooth cheeks, the sullen eyes, the rebellious thrust of the full lower lip. He said, "Been on your own long?"

The boy seemed to debate whether to answer at all. "Depends on what you call 'long,' I guess," he said finally. "I can't even remember my ma. My pa wasn't nothing to brag about, I guess. Folks that raised me said he was a gambler that followed the U.P. construction camps till he got killed in a saloon in Laramie. This family of settlers took me in to keep me from starving, but they already had a half dozen young'uns of their own. When I got big enough that I was eating a full share of the grub, the other kids made it so tough on me I finally had to pull out. I was nine then, I reckon."

"Nine!" Jim Bannister stared.

"Or ten. It's hard to keep track."

"What have you been doing all the time since?"

"I've kept alive," Clay Evans said indifferently. "Done any job I was big enough to handle—and some I wasn't. I've worked with cattle, horses. Past six months I spent with a wagon freighter hauling silver ore out of Leadville; I was his swamper, and handled the team now and again. But he busted a hip in an accident, our last trip, and that was the end of that."

"Where will you be heading now?"

"Who knows? Over the pass—that's about as far ahead as I try to see." The kid's eyes, so old and bitter in so young a face, were enough to haunt a man—and the angry rebellion in them was a troubling warning of the dangerous storms at work inside him. "Damn that Sam Murdock!" he burst out suddenly, and his knobby, work-toughened hands balled to fists. "It was all his doing! Why did he have to think he could go and act like that with me? He wasn't the first that tried it, either—but, by God, he was the last! I found out today I don't have to let anybody kick me around!"

Jim Bannister thought dryly, and you expect me to give you a gun? But neither of them mentioned that subject again.

Their scant meal finished, Bannister got up, collected the utensils, and took them out to the spring, where he rinsed them off. Afterward he settled back on his heels and looked up at the bright mesh of the stars, where a white moon was swimming now. He thought of what he had heard and wondered what this kid's chances were of working out a fair destiny.

There were the seeds of discontent and violence in him, all right—planted by a hard past and a dubious parentage, brought to fruit today in the killing of an old man. On the other hand, it must be admitted the killing hadn't been intentional, and it had only come of trying to help someone in trouble—a stranger, at that, with no claim on him except the speaking of a dozen or so halfway friendly words. The boy was plainly starved for friendship; anyone should see that, even if he chose to hide the need behind a tough veneer.

And he *had* put back that money into the till, which certainly was a good sign. Well, everybody had a load of his own to carry. Bannister shook his head, and carried his belongings back to the campfire in the rocks—where he found Clay Evans scanning, with intent interest, a piece of paper Bannister instantly recognized. As he halted in his tracks, the boy looked up; their eyes met.

"I guess you must have dropped this," Clay said dryly.

Bannister started to put a hand to his pocket, then checked the movement. "In case you're wondering," the boy said, "the answer is—yes, I can read. I done learned myself how." He slapped the paper with the back of one hand. "Mighty interesting reading, this here!"

Without comment Bannister took the reward notice out of the other's fingers. Watching him closely, Clay said, "You wanted to know my name and I told you. But you don't return the favor. I don't recall you ever saying if you really was this Jim Bannister or not."

"Hardly a thing a man would brag about, is it?" Bannister countered, looking him in the face. "Supposing it was true?"

"Twelve thousand dollars!" the boy murmured. "Old Murdock sure said it right: The law don't set such a price on a man unless they really want him bad. Or—I guess it was that Chicago syndicate put up the cash, wasn't it? That Western Development outfit?"

Bannister said curtly, "You read the notice. You know as much about it as I do."

"Yeah?" Clay Evans' teeth gleamed faintly white as his lips parted in a grin, but there was no expression mirrored in his eyes. "That's what you say. All I know is, if this Bannister gent made the mistake of killing a syndicate bigshot, he shouldn't have much to say about the mistake *I* made today. He shouldn't have anything to say at all!"

Jim Bannister felt the rebuke; his own mouth settled and went hard as he studied the black eyes in the smooth brown face. He said finally,

"You're right about one thing, anyway: It's a lot of money. But anybody who thinks about collecting it would do well to remember that a man with so much on his head would stop at nothing to keep them from doing it. He'd stop at nothing at all!"

Deliberately, Bannister folded the paper and tore it across, folded and tore it again. He dropped the pieces, fluttering, into the fire, and watched them take flame in bursts of brightness, then quickly curl, blacken, and settle into the coals.

"I'm turning in," he said, and heeled away, leaving the youngster staring at the fire with the glow of it dancing on his smooth cheeks. It made twin points of light, reflected in the dark and brooding eyes.

Bannister would have liked to see the thoughts that were hidden there.

CHAPTER IV

Mountain weather was unpredictable. Last night there'd been no hint of a change, yet when they woke the sky was heavily overcast and the higher peaks to the north of them were lost in mist. Jim Bannister was relieved to find that the sorrel appeared in better shape; it favored the hurt leg still, but examination convinced him that if he didn't press too hard, it should manage well enough.

After a hasty breakfast they saddled and packed and, leaving their camp behind, dropped again into the dim pass trail. There was no hint of travel over it during the night; that indicated the sheriff must still be behind them. So far, so good.

Now, as they climbed, the clouds settled lower and they rode into fog that obscured the ghostly pillars of the trees. Rain started. Bannister knew there was good reason to be pleased, for this would help wash their sign off the greasy surface of the trail. He broke out his slicker and put it on; Clay owned no slicker, but he did have a poncho he'd made for himself from an old square of tarp, by cutting a hole in the middle. Thus equipped, they rode on through the chill, in a continuing and uneasy silence that neither seemed inclined to break.

They crossed the pass, recognized it as such when the trail ceased to climb and leveled out, briefly, across an open upland that was barren except for a few dwarf scrub trees. Then, just as abruptly, they began to lose altitude again, and the general slope of the broken upland trended downward. The stream in the bottom of a trailside ravine ran head of them now, swollen by the rain. In another hour they were well down the northern slope of the hill barrier, and into a new region of tight valleys and piney ridges.

When the pass trail began to ravel out in a dozen separate strands, Clay Evans reined in and broke a lengthening silence. "Reckon about anywhere along here, we can split."

"Sorry. I reckon we can't."

The youngster's head lifted so sharply that rain water tunneled from a break in his hatbrim; he blinked and then his mouth drew tight. "Why the hell not?" he demanded quickly. "You're no crazier about being stuck with me than I am about being stuck with you. Oh, sure, you stood up for me with old man Murdock; but I figure I more than evened *that* score. From here on I aim to find my own way."

Jim Bannister moved his shoulders inside the shining material of the wet slicker. He said gruffly, "You ever tried running from the law before now? So far we've played in luck, especially with this rain to wash out our tracks. But if you don't know what you're doing, there's still plenty of chance to stumble into a sheriff's posse."

"That's my lookout, ain't it? You my nursemaid or something?"

"I never said so." Bannister lifted the chill, damp reins. "Just the same, I reckon I'll keep you with me a while."

He saw the kid's whole face go mean with temper. "Reckon I savvy what the facts are: I know too much about you. You're Jim Bannister, right, and you're scared to let me out of your sight. Scared I might try to collect that bounty, maybe—some time while your back is turned!"

Bannister met the insolent challenge of his stare. He took a breath and said, coldly and deliberately, "I can tell you this: I wouldn't want to have to notch my Colt on a seventeen-year-old!"

For that one moment, the matter lay clear between them—without pretense, with every bar down. It was the youngster who gave way before it. He lost some of his tough front; he blinked and his smooth cheeks paled a little. Bannister saw this with grim satisfaction. "But to finish what I started to say," he continued curtly. "We're neither of us in the clear. And if a sheriff happened to run one of us down, it would give him a pretty fair idea where to hunt the other. For my own protection, I've got to keep that from happening.

So you're trailing with me—and I wouldn't try to break and run, if I were you!"

Something in his face must have decided it. Clay's mouth tightened, and he turned away and stared grimly ahead of his roan's pointed ears; there was no more argument from him as they went on through the softly sliding rain. But the young fellow's face, with its hooded stare, was a mask of sullen hostility.

The day drew on through midmorning. They were out of the steeper hills now, into lower ridges carpeted with timber and with grass that looked as though it must be good summer graze. Bannister saw plenty of signs of cattle—well-defined stock trails threading the easier draws and rises. Once he hauled rein abruptly as a vagrant trail of woodsmoke tanged the sodden forest scent. In almost the same moment he became aware of a lowing of several head of beef.

He told the boy, "Hold it! We're coming on to something!" His caution was proved wise when, shortly afterward, the trees thinned and they halted at the edge of them, to look down upon a roundup camp directly below.

It seemed early in the season for such activity, but someone was apparently working these hills, pulling the cattle out of them. Bannister saw a camp wagon, and a tarp stretched among four treetrunks to make a shelter for a fire. Smoke spilled above the edge of the canvas, drifted in a blue haze through the pines and tanged the air that moved across the face of the hill.

Another tarp covered a pile of supplies. There were a couple of crude-looking tents. Close by, a brush gate had been thrown across the mouth of a draw to make a corral; cattle were stirring in there, hides steaming in the rain, a mingled rumble of sound rising from them. Bannister could see no human being. But he shook his head as he told Clay, "This is one place we steer clear of! Last thing either of us wants is for a sheriff to come around asking and find out somebody sighted us."

Clay nodded briefly, to show he understood and agreed. With one accord they pulled their horses back into the timber and struck out on a course that ought to take them well wide of the campfire and away from that collection herd in the brush corral.

But a roundup camp meant riders working the hills—riders they might stumble onto at almost any moment. Still, no one could drive rebellious steers out of manzanita scrub and aspen thickets without making a good deal of noise. They were on the point of jumping their horses down the bank of a shallow gully, that looked like a quick route to lower country, when they heard sounds that enabled them to hold back just in time.

Seconds later a couple of brindle-hided steers broke into the open. Hard on their heels, with a whoop and a crash, came a rider. He had no slicker and no hat. His canvas windbreaker was black with the rain; his sandy hair was plastered tight to his skull by the downpour. He carried a coil of grass rope in one hand. When one of the beef animals braked and swung around, head lowered as though to challenge him, the fellow shouted and spurred at him, swinging his rope, and the steer bellowed and turned and ran on again into the rain.

But the lariat had snagged on a pine branch overhead. It flipped out of the rider's chill fingers to the ground and he reined in, swearing, his bronc's hoofs sliding in wet forest litter as the puncher turned him back and swung off. He was just leaning to retrieve his rope when two new riders suddenly appeared around a bend of the gully.

Bannister saw them with a frown, grateful at least for the brush screen shielding the edge of the bank. He knew there was no chance of withdrawing; he and Clay Evans would simply have to hold their position and wait it out until these three decided to move on.

It looked instead as though they had unwittingly stumbled onto trouble.

Because of the thick needle cover, and the ear-filling noise of the rain, the fellow on the ground didn't seem aware of the newcomers until one of them spoke a harsh challenge: "Jackman!"

Hearing his name, he jerked erect and turned, leaving the coiled rope on the ground. When he saw the pair of horsemen he stiffened; Bannister noticed how his shoulders settled, as though he were nerving himself for a bad time. And then Bannister saw why.

Two gun muzzles were already looking at him, blue-steel barrels gleaming faintly in the dull light. "What do you want with me, Foley?" Jackman demanded.

The man who had spoken first, Foley, was a big one, a shapeless hulk of a figure in his yellow slicker. He cuffed a battered hat back on his head with one huge fist, and Bannister saw a broad face and a scurf of black, unshaven whiskers. His voice sounded surprisingly thin and nasal coming from that barrel chest.

"I reckon we've made it plain enough, what we want from you people: We want you out of these hills! We've told you, real polite, but it don't seem to do any good."

"We mind our own business. We aren't hurting you any!"

"That's what *you* say. You crowd us, mister— and us Foleys don't take to crowding. We ain't carin' for neighbors."

"That's too bad." The sandyhaired man was defiant, but his voice held an uncertain tremor.

"We're here and I don't know what you think you can do about it."

"My brother seems to think he can get rid of you with talk," big Foley answered. "Me, I'm not much good at talking. Maybe it's time I tried my own way."

Very deliberately he dropped the split reins, to hold the rawboned mountain pony ground-tied, swung a thick leg across the saddle, and stepped down. Watching, young Evans stirred uneasily on his saddle and muttered in a low voice, "Hey! What the hell's going on here?" Bannister silenced him with a gesture and a curt shake of the head. He himself was scowling, not at all liking this but determined not to interfere.

On the ground, Foley shaped up over a head taller than the other man, and he looked to be about twice as broad. Jackman could hardly be blamed if he quailed and fell back before him. Foley had shoved his gun into the holster, leaving both hands free; but his companion, a bony figure of a man who carried one shoulder higher than the other, still had the puncher covered and Jackman wouldn't have dared try for a break.

He watched as the big fellow spat deliberately into each palm and curled them into fists; he said, in a voice that didn't sound too steady, "I'm not enough of a fool to try and fight you. You know you could cut me to pieces."

49

Foley swore, and without warning one of the massive fists lashed forward. It moved with no seeming effort, yet the sheer weight of it drove Jackman's head halfway over his shoulder; it lifted him off his feet and slammed him prone. The next moment Foley was on him.

He got hold of his victim's clothing and hauled him up; the fastenings on the threadbare canvas jacket ripped loose. "Cut you to pieces, huh?" the big man said harshly. "Maybe that's just what it's going to take to teach you Jackmans the lesson!"

A shove sent the puncher spinning, stumbling headlong against a slim-boled pine tree. Jackman was still numbed by the blow and his knees sagged, refusing to hold him up. "Mitch!" the big man bawled at his companion. "Get down here, damn you. Hold him for me."

The skinny rider hurried to comply, sliding quickly off his saddle. He didn't seem to have to be told what was wanted. He went around behind the tree and pulled Jackman's arms forward around its trunk. Foley had already jerked the windbreaker completely off him; now a swipe of one big hand ripped away the fellow's shirt, baring the white skin of his back to the waist. Mitch set a boot against the treetrunk to brace himself and pulled Jackman's arms hard against the rough bark. And now Foley spread his heavy boots wide, and in his right hand was

50

the puncher's own lariat, picked up from the ground.

Bannister heard Clay Evans suck an indrawn breath as the soggy coils of rope circled and struck. The prisoner jerked convulsively but Mitch held him steady. The rope swung and slammed across his ribs a second time, a third; and now a shout of pain tore from Jackman, and there was blood on him when the rain-heavy hemp fell away.

"You only think you been hurt," Foley sneered. "You're gonna *know* it! You're gonna know it don't pay anyone to try foolin' around with us Foleys, after we-uns tell 'em to git!" The rope lifted again, circling for another slashing blow. And Jim Bannister groaned with angry frustration, certain that he would regret bitterly what he was going to have to do.

But he was already pawing away the folds of his slicker; the gun slid from his holster and, without further hesitation, he leveled it and thumbed off a shot. Lead struck the ground near one of Foley's boots; through rain and powder-smoke Bannister saw the big fellow leap in startled surprise as a gout of damp pine needles exploded. After that Bannister was kicking the sorrel forward, shoul-dering past Clay Evans' bronc and jumping him down into the gully.

Seen closer up, the big man was brutish, thick-featured, no great intelligence showing in the piggish eyes that scowled at Bannister as the latter reined in. He stood with his arm still lifted as though ready for another blow, the coils of yellow rope dangling.

He said, with savage harshness, "Were you shooting at me?"

"If I'd shot at you," Bannister told him bluntly, "be damn sure I wouldn't have hit the ground. That was just a warning. Now tell your friend to let this man go."

"Hell with you!" bawled Foley, and with a quickness Jim Bannister wouldn't have expected from him he suddenly whipped that coiled rope across the space between them. Unluckily it caught the front sight of Bannister's gun and sent it spinning; at once Foley had dropped the lariat and was pawing for the holster strapped to his own slabby thigh.

Bannister couldn't let him get hold of a gun. Without hesitation he launched himself bodily from the saddle, hands reaching. He collided with Foley; air gushed from the man's thick chest and his gun, just clearing leather, popped out of his fingers. Then he went down and Bannister went with him; they struck the ground solidly, under the combined weight of two big men.

It was probably not often that Foley ran up against an opponent to match him, but he had nearly such a match in big Jim Bannister, though even Bannister would have to give him perhaps twenty pounds of muscle strung on that outsized frame. But with all his advantage, the man recognized no niceties of fighting ethics. Bannister felt fingers groping toward his eyes, and when he turned his head aside the nails ripped hot pain down his cheek.

He struck at the massive jaw. His knuckles scraped beard stubble and then Foley managed, with an upward thrust of his body, to throw Bannister's weight off him. After that they were rolling in the wet and stony litter that covered the gully's floor. Bannister's opponent tried for his throat, but he chopped the hand aside. A knee, aimed at his groin, caught his thigh muscle instead with a force that nearly paralyzed it.

Thoroughly angered now, if he hadn't been before, Bannister found an opening and drove his fist solidly, twice, into the exposed face below him. Foley's lips smashed and Bannister felt his knuckle scored against the edge of a tooth. A groan broke from the man and for that moment his muscles seemed to lose their resilience; and Bannister, breaking free, stumbled up from the ground. Panting, he leaned and got Foley by the stiff material of his slicker and dragged him up onto his knees.

The big man swung at him and missed. Mouth grim, Bannister deliberately clubbed him again in his bloody face and then, as a great shudder went all through the man, let him drop; but even now, Foley wasn't completely knocked out. He found the strength somewhere to get his hands against the ground, and crouched like that, with head hanging and the blood dripping from his mouth.

Bannister swiped a sleeve across his own wet cheeks and, remembering the big fellow's companion, turned quickly. He was relieved to find that Mitch had been taken care of. Caught off guard by the sudden violence, he'd apparently let himself be surprised and disarmed by his own prisoner. Jackman had the gun and Mitch, both hands lifted, offered no fight at all.

To the sandyhaired man Bannister said, "He hurt you bad with that rope, friend?"

"Not too bad." Jackman shrugged bared shoulders. "But if you hadn't stopped him I reckon he'd have stripped my hide. Thanks!"

Bannister only nodded. Seeing his hat on the ground, he stooped and picked it up. The gun Foley had knocked from his hand lay nearby and he got that too. Then, belatedly, he remembered Clay Evans and whirled for a look at the bank of the gully, expecting to see it empty.

If it had been himself, anxious as he knew the boy was to get away, he wouldn't have wasted this opportunity. But no, the kid was still there, sitting his saddle as though petrified by what he had seen going on in front of him. Too late he seemed aware of the chance he had missed.

He gave a start, the roan's head jerking under the pull of the reins.

Bannister let the barrel of the gun swing toward him, almost casually, and sent his voice pleasantly across the sudden stillness: "Don't go away, kid. Come on down. The trouble's over."

CHAPTER V

Clay Evans glared at him, and at the gun. He appeared about to defy the order. But then, in surly anger, he gave his horse a kick that sent it sliding down the bank. As he did, a slur of hoofbeats on pine needles announced new arrivals; it pulled Bannister quickly around to watch them come toward him. One was an old man, a harmless-looking fellow with sad eyes and a beaten look about him, and a straggling fall of whiskers he wore whacked off a few inches below his lantern jaw.

It was the girl, though, who held Bannister's eye after she had got near enough for him to see she *was* a girl. She wore jeans and an old hat and what looked like a man's coat, sizes too big for her—like the sandyhaired Jackman, neither of the new-comers seemed to own a slicker. Brown hair had been tucked up out of the way, under the hat's broken brim; the column of her throat, revealed by the unbuttoned shirt collar, looked delicate and almost fragile. She was breathing quickly with excitement.

"We heard a shot," the girl exclaimed; her words broke off as she took in the situation—the stranger, and the big man on his knees. She stared at Bannister, incredulous. "Mister, did you really whup Hack Foley? I never thought *anybody* could do that!"

"It wasn't easy," Bannister admitted, and touched his cheek that burned from the rip of the big man's nails.

The old fellow with the whiskers was peering anxiously at young Jackman. "What happened?" he demanded.

"They jumped me, Pa. Hack said he was gonna make an example of me, and then he started to work me over with my own lass rope!"

Mitch broke in hastily, sweating as he eyed the gun in his face. "Don't look at *me!* I only follow orders. I never knew what Hack had in mind."

"Oh, no!" Bannister retorted. "You just held him good and steady so the rope wouldn't miss!" To young Jackman he added, "It marked you up some. You'd better put something on those cuts."

"Let me see," the girl said quickly, and started to knee her pony over to have a look; but Jackman moved away, shaking his head in protest— embarrassed, was Jim Bannister's guess.

"It's nothing," he said gruffly. "I'm all right."

Now Hack Foley came lunging to his feet, the material of his yellow slicker crackling. He passed the back of a hand across his mashed lips, saw the blood on his knuckles and swore.

"Don't think this changes anything!" he said. "We ran the other guy off, the one that first tried to move in here with them Spur cattle. We can do it again."

The girl flared back, no sign of fear in her. "Go ahead, make your big, tough talk! We ain't scared! We know our rights; and it'll take more than anything you've done yet to get rid of us!"

"Whatever it takes, you'll get it—don't worry. And don't never say you wasn't warned!"

Hack Foley let his piggish stare include young Jackman and the old man. Then, with a summoning jerk of his head at Mitch, he turned away to his waiting horse—a big bay animal, with stocky legs designed to bear the load he put on it. He was groping for the stirrup when he remembered something; laying a hand on his empty holster, under the slicker, he turned and started to search the ground.

Bannister said quietly, "You get the gun later, Foley. Just leave it."

"Like hell!" the big fellow exploded, his head whipping around. But when he saw the weapon in Bannister's hand, trained squarely on him, his eyes seemed to change color slightly and his cheeks bunched with tight muscle. "We ever cross trails again," he said, "you just watch out!"

He turned, found the stirrup and swung up; his tremendous weight strained the cinches and dragged the wet saddle far over before he settled squarely into the leather. His smaller companion, Mitch, had already scrambled onto his own mount. They kicked their horses into motion and, not once looking back, rode on down the gully and out of sight. The sound of their passage faded.

Jackman let out his breath in a long sigh. "Well, now we know! They aren't just bluffing. From here on we better all start carrying guns on our saddles. That includes you, Tansy," he told the girl.

"Those savages!" the girl exclaimed. "We got us a deal to work these hills for Spur cattle, and they can't stop us!"

"Was that your roundup camp I saw?" Bannister asked. "Over west a quarter mile?"

"That's right. Jackman's our name." She leaned from the saddle and offered him a hard little paw of a hand. "I'm Tansy Jackman. These here are my uncle El and my cousin Noah."

Bannister took the hand; belying the first impression of delicacy, it was strong and firm in his own engulfing fingers. Uncomfortable, because he didn't enjoy lying to her, he spoke the first name that came to mind: "I'm Jim Ward. The kid yonder is my nephew Billy."

She acknowledged the introduction with a nod, and a smile for the boy, which Clay Evans ignored, his scowl unchanged.

"You from one of the other hill ranches?"

"No. More or less drifting, I guess you'd call it." Bannister indicated, vaguely, the country westward. "We were heading for Downey. Someone told us to look for a pass, but looks like we missed it somewhere."

"Looks like you must of," Noah Jackman said. "I can show you the pass trail, though."

His father, the old fellow Tansy called Uncle El, said soberly, "You'd best be getting those cuts tended to, before you try doing anything else. I think there's some stuff in the wagon that'll help."

"I'm all right," Noah insisted, though he winced as he slipped his arms into the torn jacket Bannister held for him.

To Bannister, Tansy suggested, "Why don't you two come to the wagon with us? It's near time for chow right now."

Uncle El agreed. "Sure, why not? You're more than welcome."

"Well—I don't know."

He hesitated and looked over at Clay. It was hard to think of an excuse to refuse their hospitality; and the idea of a fire and warm food, and perhaps a tarp shelter to keep off the monotonous, eroding beat of drizzling rain while he took time to eat, was tempting.

"All right," Bannister said. "I guess we could use some hot grub, at that. If you're sure you've got plenty. . . ."

The food was fine—beef stew and black coffee, and biscuits out of the dutch oven buried in the coals. Fingers of rain drummed on the tarp overhead. It was crowded under there, with an occasional gust of wind along the slope scattering the trapped smoke of the fire among them and setting them all to coughing; but it was pleasant to feel the heat start to take the chill out of wet clothing.

Jim Bannister asked some questions and learned more about these Jackmans. They were from Wyoming, a hard-luck family who had run a brand of their own up on the northern ranges until trouble descended on them in the form of a dispute with the powerful cattle barons. Peacefully inclined, not at all fighters, the Jackmans hadn't been equal to such pressures; when they were driven out, stripped of most of their possessions, they had left one or two dead—including Tansy's own father—in shallow and hastily marked graves. Uncle El's wife had died in the course of their lonely and hopeless trek in search of a new place to light. The sad old man's eyes misted and his shrunken mouth trembled as he spoke of her.

Now there were just these left—a shabby, poverty-stricken outfit. Uncle El was the nominal head, but Jim Bannister suspected the girl was the one who hadn't had her spirit beaten down by the cruelty of events.

"What about these Foleys?" Bannister wanted to know. "They really think they can hold all this stretch of hill country for themselves?"

"They've done a pretty good job up to now," she told him. "There's three of them—three brothers, and a crew to match. Hack may be the biggest, but he's not the most dangerous; that'd be Jed—the brains of the outfit. Hack's nothing but bone and muscle."

"They have a spread somewhere around here, do they?"

"Back in the hills," Uncle El said. "Just north and west of us. It's supposed to be a stock ranch, but most people are pretty sure the only stock they raise is what they lift off their neighbors. Most people, though, are too scared of them to make an issue of it, so the sheriff's office leaves well enough alone. Besides, it's a pretty piddlin' kind of operation, in most cases. But now, look here!"

He turned and pointed to the collection herd, beyond the brush fence. "You can see for yourself how many Spurs we've managed to chouse out of the timber in almost two weeks' trying. Book count shows there ought to be two, three times this many. After they scared Ed Haslon out of the country, they must have figured anything carrying a Spur was fair game. Probably would have had it all, I reckon—except they didn't figure anybody else would actually get up the nerve to come in and try to work this brand. Not so soon, at least."

Uncle El wagged his head slowly, the chopped-off whiskers brushing his shirt front. "Until today, they never done more to us than pass a few threats. Looks like they're moving beyond threatening now."

"This Ed Haslon," Bannister said, after a moment. "I take it that's the man you're working for?"

"Oh, no. Our deal's with the man he sold out to. It looked like a good chance, for a bunch of people down on their luck. We didn't even know about the Foleys until after we'd agreed to take it on."

Tansy Jackman said stoutly, "It's *still* a good deal! We just have to stand up and show 'em we ain't to be scared out. And once we get this herd into shape, and prove we're able to run Spur— then we got Mr. Murdock's promise to let us take over half ownership of the ranch."

Jim Bannister's head jerked sharply. "Murdock?"

She nodded. "He's not a cattleman; he runs a store, over on the other side of the pass. So you see, he's got to have somebody up here that knows about managing a cow spread."

There was still food on Bannister's tin plate, but he was suddenly no longer hungry. He lowered plate and fork, appalled; his throat clogged for a moment with unspoken words. "You got all this down in writing, I hope? Signed and witnessed?"

Blank looks met his question, and confirmed

his worst suspicions. Finally Uncle El said, "Well, now, I've always figured a man's word should be good."

"Yeah," Bannister said, a little grimly. "It *should* be. . . ." For a moment he found himself struggling under almost intolerable pressures. These people had every right to hear of the death of Sam Murdock; it was important they should hear. And yet, he'd told too many lies to contradict himself now with the truth. He'd already denied ever having been across the pass, so there was no legitimate way for him to have known anything at all about Murdock. Debating the problem, he glanced over at Clay Evans and caught the boy staring at him with a look of apprehension. The boy's eyes begged him to hold his tongue.

"It's a big job," Uncle El commented, as Bannister failed to speak, "for folks in our position. We're shorthanded, even with Tansy doing a man's share of the work." His glance settled on Bannister speculatively. "But say, now! Wouldn't so happen you'd be looking for work—you and the boy here? We could sure use some help the next month or so. Though you might have to wait a little for your pay. . . ."

"No!" Tansy protested, throwing a reproachful look at her uncle. "It wouldn't be right, expecting him to ask for more trouble from them Foleys. It ain't fair even to suggest it!"

The old man accepted the reprimand meekly enough. "Reckon I just didn't think," he admitted. "Forget I said anything, Jim." But his eyes continued to hold Bannister's hopefully; and the girl's, too, held such warmth and open friendliness that his sense of guilt increased and he felt a sudden need to escape.

He said lamely, "I don't know. We had other plans. I'll have to think it over." Minutes later, thanking them again for the meal, he laid his empty plate aside and crawled from beneath the tarp—to have a look, he said, at the bronc's hurt leg.

The steady rain, after its long hours of soaking the forest and the hills, had finally ended and the clouds were beginning to break. A dazzle of sunlight came through, bringing color to the wet world: drops of moisture sparkled and trembled on a million pine needles, made a dripping, runneling music through the afternoon stillness. Bannister walked over to where the horses were tied, still under saddle, in the half shelter of a small stand of trees. On checking the sorrel's tender foreleg, he was satisfied to discover that the day's travel seemed not to have affected it. As he straightened again, he heard a footstep behind him and someone spoke the name he had given these people: "Ward!" He turned to find Noah Jackman facing him.

The sandyhaired man had said little during the

meal, but had sat silently apart; Bannister thought the pain of his hurt shoulder, despite the careful job of bandaging by his cousin Tansy, must have made him moody.

Now, as Noah looked up at the big stranger, his eyes were hooded and there was a tight and troubled set to his mouth.

Bannister said, "Something I can do for you?"

"Yeah." Noah swallowed, with an effort. "You can climb on that horse and get out of here!"

Bannister's head jerked with surprise at this man's vehemence. He frowned. "You don't like me much, do you?"

"I got nothing against you," Noah answered doggedly. "How the hell could I? You saved me from a beating, and maybe worse. But, mister, that's all we *do* know about you. And I see the way Tansy looks at you! I'd rather take a dozen beatings from Hack Foley than watch some stranger drop in here and maybe do her hurt."

"I see." Bannister did, too; a good many things were beginning to fall into place. "I take it you're in love with her. Your own cousin. . . ."

"We ain't related," Noah Jackman corrected him. "Even if we do have the same name. The old man is her uncle, but he's only my step-father. Sure, I love her!" he added defensively. "Though I never told her. I know there's nothing flashy about me. I ain't much on looks, and you could likely break me in two. But, by God, I'll kill the man that causes her grief!"

His jaws were set, his voice a tight whisper; the glitter of his eyes was enough to show the feverish sincerity inside this man. Bannister looked at him for a long moment, and felt his temper slipping.

"You're jumping at conclusions," he said coldly. "Maybe I better give you a little advice: If what you feel is as strong as all that, I suggest you talk to *her*—don't try to scare strangers off. Because somebody just might come along and decide to call your bluff!"

Jackman stiffened; his cheeks lost color, and then a swift tide of red swept over them. He drew in a sharp breath between set teeth and reached a hand as though he would seize the bigger man's coat front.

Whatever might have been said next was lost, for Jim Bannister's interest was suddenly jarred by the sight of Clay Evans hurrying through the trees directly to the place where the roan was tied. As he saw the boy reach for the reins and jerk loose the knot that held them to a pine branch, Bannister called sharply, "Boy, where do you think you're going?"

The youngster gave him no more than a look, but it was eloquent enough. He vaulted into saddle without touching stirrup, and the roan stepped quickly back as he jerked the rein. At the same moment Bannister heard a sound of approaching horses. He paused in the act of moving a step toward Clay, with the intention of hauling him bodily from the back of the roan if he had to; he halted, and turned, and looked. What he saw answered his question for him: Two horsemen were coming in, moving at a canter through the steaming sunshine. Their faces were undistinguishable below pulled hatbrims. What held Bannister's stare was the glint of sunlight reflected from metal pinned to the calfskin vest of one of them.

He knew a lawman when he saw one.

CHAPTER VI

As he stood motionless, in indecision, he heard the quick beat of the kid's horse starting away through the trees behind him. All the uneasiness in the presence of the law, ingrained by his months of running from it, welled up, and he had to quell the impulse to throw himself into his own saddle. But that would gain him nothing; from Noah Jackman's suspicious stare, Bannister knew it would be all the man needed to make him raise a shout of alarm.

He would have to brazen it out. At least, he thought, by stalling I may be able to give the kid a chance. . . . With Noah's hostile eyes on him, he took time to settle his breathing and then walked out of the trees, bearing toward the lawmen with a stride that suggested nothing more than simple curiosity.

The newcomers had dismounted and Tansy Jackman and her uncle had both joined them, walking over from the direction of the fire. The sheriff, the larger of the two men—the other appeared to be a deputy—was already explaining his business, in a blunt and carrying voice that reached across the stillness.

"Thought you might have noticed a stranger.

We're pretty sure he came over the pass last night, but that rain washed out his sign."

"What would he look like?" Uncle El wanted to know.

"Supposed to be a big fellow, maybe six-three or four. Yellow hair, pale eyes. There's a chance he's traveling with a surly, black-headed kid of seventeen or so—at least, the kid's turned up missing. . . ." The lawman's voice trailed off. He caught sight of Bannister, nearing the group; as his glance ranged the length of the big man, his whole body stiffened. "Who's this, Jackman?"

Almost as though by accident, the sheriff's hand had moved to the grip of the wooden-handled gun in his holster. He was not really an old man—his tight cap of woolly hair, visible below the hatbrim, was barely touched with gray—but his face had sun-darkened and weathered into a mass of wrinkles that spread from the corners of his eyes, creased his forehead, and bracketed his mouth, and conveyed every faintest shift of emotion. Bannister saw the varying shades of suspicion reflected in that expressive face and in the steady probe of slate-gray eyes; it seemed to him an endless time that he stood waiting for the ax to fall.

And then Tansy Jackman, with the faintest tremor in her voice, was saying, "Oh, don't you know Jim, Mr. Parrott? This is Jim Ward. He works for us."

The sheriff's sharp glance shot to her. "Works for you? Since when?"

"He came down from Wyoming with us. He's been with us right along. I thought you met him that day in town."

Listening to her lie with such glib efficiency, Bannister could only stare—and he saw that the sheriff was staring, too. He thought surely somebody was going to blow the thing wide open; but apparently Tansy knew her relatives. Neither man said anything—not even Noah Jackman, who stood to one side with a thunderous scowl listening to the girl he loved lying for the stranger he counted a rival.

The sheriff turned back to the tall man, his stare unyielding. "Lucky there was someone to speak for you, mister," he said, in a voice that struck Bannister as being freighted with double meaning. "From your looks, you sure could have been our man!" The same veiled distrust was reflected on the face of the one who stood beside him, a deputy's badge pinned to his corduroy jacket.

Uncle El shifted scuffed jackboots, pawed at his chopped-off whiskers. "Who is this fellow you're looking for, Sheriff?" he demanded gruffly. "What's he wanted for?"

"Murder!" the lawman answered in the bluntest of tones. "His name's Bannister, and there's a reward out for him that would knock your eyes

71

out. He stopped at Sam Murdock's store yesterday, and Sam recognized him from a dodger and put a gun on him. But Bannister killed him and got away."

"*Killed* him?" Noah Jackman exclaimed. "Killed Sam Murdock?"

Seeing the stunned look that came into Tansy's face, it was all that Jim Bannister could do to keep from breaking out with a quick denial.

"Killed him dead," Parrott said crisply. "That's the way it looks, anyhow. Bert and me—" he indicated the deputy—"we were out of town on a job, didn't hear about it or take the trail till this morning. But the men that investigated found Murdock lying dead in his own blood. Bannister was gone. Only one who might know what happened was that kid I mentioned; and, like I said, he's disappeared. Bannister may have killed him, too, for all anybody knows."

"But—Murdock!" Uncle El couldn't get past this one stunning fact. "Dead! Why, it can't be! What—what's it gonna do to *us?*"

"Say, that's right!" the sheriff exclaimed. "I almost forgot. You were working for Sam, weren't you?"

"We had a deal; we were to put this property into shape and then, if it panned out, take over a partnership arrangement. We been working our heads off! What do you think will happen to our deal now?"

The lawman took off his hat, ran a hand

across his woolly cap of hair. "I suppose you got something on paper? Properly witnessed?"

It was the second time Uncle El had heard that question. He shook his head. "No papers, no witness. We just talked things over and came to an agreement."

"Then, in that case, I'm afraid you may be in for a little trouble. Claude Pine, the lawyer over to Downey, is the one to tell you. Of course, maybe if you're lucky you can make terms with Murdock's sister; she'll be inheriting. Pine told me this morning he'd sent her a wire and is expecting her in the next day or two. If I were you I'd hold tight until you can talk to her and thresh this whole thing out."

"What kind of a woman is this sister?" Noah Jackman wanted to know.

"As to that, I couldn't say. I never met her."

There was a long silence. Bannister could feel the weight of disheartened anxiety that had settled in these Jackmans. Then, slowly, one by one, their glances lifted and sought his face; he read the same cold and silent accusation in them all. All but Tansy Jackman. Though he steeled himself to meet her eyes, she kept them lowered; but her hands were twisted together until the knuckles showed white.

It was the deputy, Bert, who broke the stillness. He was a mild-mannered man in his thirties, with a homely, honest face. He shifted his boots and said tentatively, "Well, Sid, if there's nothing more we can do here—"

Sid Parrott stood unyielding. He said, "Would there be any java left in that pot yonder?"

"Why sure!" Uncle El agreed quickly, stirring himself. "There's stew and biscuits, too. Tansy, fix these fellows up.

"Hope you won't mind if we go on about our business? Maybe it's all a waste of time, after this—but it's no good dropping a job in the middle, especially with the day only half done."

"Go right ahead," the sheriff said, with a wave of the hand. "No need to wait on us. Bert and I can manage."

The scene broke apart, the lawmen leading their horses over to the trees and tying, then returning to duck beneath the tarp and begin serving up grub and coffee for themselves. The Jackmans, with the trancelike and wooden movements of those who had seen the bottom knocked out of their world, prepared to get back to work. Getting ready to mount, himself, Jim Bannister cast a glance toward the fire and suddenly froze; he saw Sid Parrott, cup and plate steaming in his hands, narrowly listening to something he was being told by Noah Jackman.

This is it! Bannister thought; it was too much to have hoped the fellow would hold his tongue for long, eaten as he was by jealousy. He dragged in a deep breath and, choosing to meet disaster head on, started walking directly toward the fire. He led the sorrel, his right hand carefully swinging free.

And then he heard Noah speak the name: "Foley." And he realized he had misjudged the nature of this conversation. He halted.

The sheriff was saying, "Let me understand you. You want to prefer charges against Hack Foley?"

"No, no." Noah shook his head. "What happened this morning was a personal matter; I just thought you should know. Because I serve notice right now that if they keep their threats—or hurt any more of this family—I expect the law to do something!" He added bluntly, "I'm wondering why nothing's been done before. You've known what was going on in these hills."

Bannister saw anger move across Sid Parrott's expressive features; the sheriff reddened a little. He said crisply, "Knowing and proving are two different things. The law can't work miracles, you know. It can only move a step at a time."

"A step at a time!" the sandyhaired man repeated, and lifted his shoulders irritably. His lips worked over some further angry retort, but he left it unspoken. Instead, he merely turned and tramped away.

Bannister let out trapped breath, glad to see the last of that exchange. Looking around, he saw Tansy Jackman, already mounted, and caught the look she threw him—the small but imperiously summoning gesture of her head. He nodded, and found the stirrup. As he rose into saddle and touched spurs to his horse, he looked again at the lawmen settling down comfortably at the fire, tin cups and plates of hot food steaming in their laps; he could feel their eyes following him, until the screen of timber came between.

The girl was waiting. She put her own pony beside his and they rode on at a walk, to a scuff of iron shoes on pine litter, with the tree shadows and shafting sunlight flickering over them; Bannister looked at her and saw that her expression was bleak and grim. She said finally, "Where's the boy?"

"I don't know. He took off when he saw the sheriff." He hesitated. "You saved me from a bad time, back there. I want to thank you."

She continued to look straight ahead of her, at her pony's ears. "You *are* Bannister, aren't you? You're the man Sid Parrott's looking for?"

"I'm Jim Bannister. I've got a price on my head, and a couple of bounty hunters trailing me—though I think I lost them somewhere, a hundred miles back. Right now, your sheriff is no more than half convinced by what you told him, yet he isn't ready to come right out and accuse you folks of lying. What I don't see is how you could be so sure the rest of them would back you up." He thought he did know, though. He had already guessed that Tansy Jackman, with her forthright and stubborn nature, was really the dominant member in her family of males.

She dismissed the matter with a shrug. She said, in the same heavy tone, "And you killed Sam Murdock. Or are you going to deny that you know anything about it?"

"I was there, but I didn't kill him. It was—" He thought of Clay Evans, defiant and scared and friendless, and he didn't have it in him to finish. "It was an accident," he ended, knowing it sounded lame.

That answer brought her eyes to him, and she studied him gravely for a long minute as their horses moved on through the hillside timber. When she looked away again he couldn't be sure whether she believed him or not. She said in a weary tone, "However it happened, it couldn't have been any worse for us."

"I'm not so sure of that," he said bluntly. "If it hadn't happened you might have gone on like this, putting in months of work and trying to hold your own with the Foleys, only to find yourselves out in the cold."

"I don't understand."

"I saw a sample of the way Murdock operated. He was the kind who'd take advantage of anyone that wasn't in a position to make him honor his terms. Sure, maybe he'd have given you folks a decent settlement for your efforts; but again, maybe he wouldn't. Not without something legal in writing to bind him."

He saw the girl's jaw set stubbornly. "If that's what he was up to, it's one time he didn't know who he was dealing with!" But then her mouth began to work and her eyes shone with tears. "Oh, Jim! What are we going to do?" she cried miserably. "We've been kicked around just once too often. I think this time it will about kill Uncle El."

There was nothing, really, to say. All he could manage was, "I'm sorry. I only wish I knew what to tell you."

Suddenly her thoughts returned to him, with the breathtaking swiftness she had. She pulled her pony to a standstill as she turned to face him, anxious and intense. "And you, Jim Bannister? The sheriff said it's another murder you're wanted for. . . ."

"A syndicate man." Bannister nodded. "Him I killed, but it wasn't murder. Still, it's a long story, and it doesn't have to concern you. I'm not begging you to believe me."

Her eyes studied him. "All I know," she answered finally, "is that you're in trouble now because you stepped in to save my cousin Noah from a beating. We owe you something." She turned and glanced quickly back through the trees. "This is your chance. Ride for it, while you can. I'll try to cover with the sheriff."

He shook his head. "Thanks for even suggesting it, Tansy, but it wouldn't work. Sid Parrott's stalling, like as not just waiting to see if I'll give myself away by trying to run for it. I doubt if he'd let me get far."

"But what are you going to do?"

"I don't know yet. Try to wait him out, I suppose. And if I can't get him thinking he's guessed wrong—well, I should have better luck making a break once it gets dark." He might have added, but didn't, assuming that one of the others doesn't decide to give me away in the meantime.

Tansy looked a little dubious herself, but she didn't argue. And Bannister, giving the sorrel a kick, said, "Come on. We're supposed to be looking for cattle."

CHAPTER VII

It soon became evident that all this section, within easy radius of the camp, had been thoroughly combed already. Bannister knew the intention had been to finish up here today and move the collection herd out of that draw, down onto graze near ranch headquarters; tomorrow, the Jackmans had planned to move their camp to another quarter and begin the job anew. But now there would be little point in that—not until they could find out just what Sam Murdock's death meant to them, and where they stood.

By a lucky chance, Bannister and the girl jumped a fair-sized jag of Spur stock in a natural pocket of graze that had somehow been overlooked. They went in and got them out; and in the blood-warming activity of working reluctant cattle, Tansy Jackman seemed to lose some of her moodiness. Obviously she was a real cowhand, sitting her saddle and maneuvering the pony with reckless skill and an open zest for this kind of thing. As for Bannister, there was real pleasure in being able to give himself again, if only for an hour, to the healthy activity of range work.

But they were both sobered quickly enough as, laughing over something Bannister had said, they hazed their jag of steers toward the collection herd and saw the sheriff and his deputy still lounging near the fire. Their meal was finished and now the two were enjoying a smoke, clearly in no hurry to be about their business. Their eyes followed Bannister with a cold intensity. After the steers had been put into the pen, some streak of audacity made him ride over there and deliberately swing down to help himself to coffee. They watched in silence as he returned the battered pot to the coals and then drank.

"You're burnin' daylight, Sheriff," he remarked chidingly, eying Parrott over the rim of the cup. "You figure to catch up with your man this way?"

Sid Parrott squinted up at him, standing silhouetted against the sun. "Maybe I figure if I wait long enough he'll walk right up to me."

"Murderers aren't usually that obliging, are they?"

The sheriff took the cigarette from his lips, looked at the way it was burning. "I'm beginning to think this one's no usual sort of a murderer."

"From what I've heard," Bannister said, "sounds like you can just about bet on one thing: If he's ever cornered, he won't be taken without a fight."

"Oh. Then you've heard of him? I didn't know."

"I've heard of him."

Tansy Jackman had reined in at a little distance and was watching all this, worrying her lip with her teeth, uneasy and exasperated. She called suddenly, "Jim! Are you coming?"

"Sure." He finished his coffee, spilled the dregs on the ground, and tossed the cup into the wreck pan. He looked a moment longer at the sheriff. "Well, good luck. . . ."

When Bannister joined her, Tansy turned to him a face that was reproachful, and pale with alarm. "Should you needle him like that?" she exclaimed in a fierce whisper. "You'll only make things worse!"

"They couldn't be much worse." His eyes, as he looked back at the fire, were bleakly thoughtful. "I know what he's doing: He's trying to pressure me into making some move that will give me away. He wouldn't be acting like that if he wasn't pretty damned sure I'm his man. And yet he won't act."

"If you're saying Sid Parrott is a coward—I don't believe it!"

"Not a coward, maybe. But cautious. And sometimes a cautious man can be bluffed."

She started to say something more but, whatever it might have been, it was never spoken. For at that moment the first gunshot sounded.

It broke across the stillness and lifted Bannister in his stirrups. Another shot followed, then a scattered firing, and suddenly he became aware of a rumble of moving hoofs and a protesting bellow in the throats of frightened cattle. His head swiveled just in time to see a mass of beef strike the improvised brush gate across the mouth of the draw.

It withstood the first thrust, cracking and bulging but flinging back the cattle as they tried to break through. But, by the second thrust, panic was rising. The mass of meat and muscle struck again, and this time the whole fence seemed to explode outward into broken splinters. The frightened brutes came streaming out.

Even these few head could do a lot of damage, once they started running. Bannister looked for Tansy Jackman and found her sitting motionless, as though stunned. He shouted something, and when she didn't answer he reached and got her pony by the bridle, as he kicked his own sorrel forward. He ran both horses to safety up a slight rise of ground, with mud spurting under their hoofs, and there he turned back to look at what was happening.

He had a glimpse of the sheriff scrambling out of the way; then the tide of flesh hit the fire and brought down the tarp shelter. It ran over the tents and flattened them. The camp wagon took a sideswiping blow that slewed it around but left it standing. And as quickly as that, it was over. The stampede passed and vanished in scrub brush and timber, leaving behind a swath of trampled earth and the wreckage of what had been a roundup camp.

Tansy Jackman was sobbing with fury. "It was the Foleys!" she cried. "They're the only ones could have done this. Oh, damn them! All our work. . . ."

Bannister didn't even hear her. He had dropped Tansy's bridle, pulled his revolver; not pausing to debate the sense of what he was doing, he gave his horse a spur and sent it pounding toward the mouth of the draw where the herd had been held.

Rocks and trampled earth steamed in rising tendrils. He jumped the wreckage of the brush fence and beyond, past a narrow entrance, saw the draw widen to make a very fair holding ground, with graze and sufficient water. Bannister rode straight ahead, recklessly, and was rewarded by a glimpse of a horseman drifting across the line of his travel. From the size, it looked very much like Hack Foley.

With the knowledge that Tansy Jackman could as easily as not have been caught under that destructive rush of knife-sharp hoofs, Bannister dropped his gun barrel and triggered through the wavering curtain of steam. The rider ran on, and Bannister lost him. He spurred in pursuit.

Moments later he was pulling up when a gun somewhere to his right roared. He heard the whip of the bullet, saw the flash of muzzleflame out of the corner of an eye. That gun was close, and he knew well enough the kind of target he made in the saddle; he needed no further warning to bring him quickly to the ground. There, shielded by the lunging body of the sorrel, he laid his gun wrist across the saddle and fired twice.

A horse squealed, stung by a bullet. Through the burst of powdersmoke he saw the animal rear; as its rider fought it down, he glimpsed black eyes in a hawkish face. That other gun flamed a second time, and he ducked instinctively. The bullet struck his saddlehorn a glancing blow, the force of it driving the sorrel stumbling against him and nearly putting him off his feet.

Recovered, he searched, but the rider was gone. So was Hack Foley. Finding himself suddenly alone, Bannister spoke to the sorrel to settle it, and swung astride again; but after that he held where he was, scowling. "This is ridiculous," he muttered under his breath. "What do I think I'm proving?"

But then, somewhere, running hoofs threw back a spatter of sound, beating off some stretch of exposed rock. At once, without even thinking, he was again kicking the sorrel into a run.

At its upward end, the draw broke against a crumbling clay wall and he saw where the shod hoofs of several horses had partly broken down the rain-wet clay. Rubble, dislodged by the steel of Foley mounts, was still spilling down the steep slant as Bannister put the sorrel after them.

The footing was loose and treacherous; twice his mount tried it, and twice the animal floundered back. Then it got purchase and scrambled to the top and over. Bannister sent it down an easy slant, into a trough of naked rock that had sent back the spatter of echoing hoofsound he had heard moments earlier. Quitting this, he rode out onto a bench where timber slants fell away in two directions. He could see no movement, and heard nothing at all except the heavy breathing of his own horse.

Suddenly the sorrel stumbled under him and he pulled up, remembering belatedly that he couldn't use that strained left foreleg too hard. He laid a hand on the bronc's neck, felt the sweat streaming. "Sorry, fellow," he said. "I forgot!" Sign of the previous riders showed clearly, pointing ahead, but he gave it little more than a look, since pursuit was now out of the question.

He sat for a moment, listening to the silence and letting the tired horse breathe while he pulled his gun and thumbed fresh shells from his belt loops to replace the ones he had burned. Afterward, holstering the weapon, he turned and rode slowly back the way he had come.

The instant he was in sight of the roundup camp, and saw the cluster of people gathered about something lying on the torn ground, he knew that more than tents and camp equipment had been damaged in that raid. The hurt man was Bert, the deputy. He lay quite still, his eyes closed. Sid Parrot knelt by him, and Bannister heard the sheriff saying, in a bitter voice, "I saw him stumble, and they rolled right over him! Looks like his leg and a couple of ribs. Maybe worse. . . ."

The lawman straightened slowly to his feet. He lifted a hand, rubbed it over his oddly wrinkled face. "There was nothing much dangerous about Bert Grinstead," he went on, speaking to the girl and to her uncle El, who stood beside her. "He was just a guy trying to support a wife and a couple of kids on the salary I was able to pay him. But, by God," he said hoarsely, "if I've brought him out here and got him killed on account of some no-good bastard of a murderer—"

He broke off; his eyes had speared Bannister as the latter rode out of the draw and came to an uneasy stand. For a moment Bannister thought that, in his anger, Sid Parrott was about to forget caution and pull a gun on him. He waited, giving him every chance. But when the moment passed and the sheriff made no move, Bannister said into the stillness, "If your man dies, it's the Foleys who killed him."

The eyes that studied him were without expression now. "There was more shooting, a minute ago. Was that you?"

Bannister nodded curtly. "I spotted Hack Foley and another man I didn't happen to recognize. My sorrel was too near played out to let me follow the trail they left."

The sheriff turned and for a long moment stared off in the direction of the draw. He looked at the man lying unconscious at his feet, and then raised his eyes again to Bannister. He said crisply, "Show me!"

"If you say so. But I'll have to borrow a horse."

"You can take his." As Bannister dismounted, the sheriff turned to Uncle El and the girl. "Do what you can for him," he ordered, indicating the hurt man. "We'll be back."

They nodded silently. Sid Parrott moved off at a flatfooted run toward the trees, where Bannister was already lifting into the deputy's saddle, not troubling to adjust the stirrups. The sheriff mounted and fell in beside him, and they spurred away into the draw.

They rode fast and silently. When they reached the bench where he had been forced to turn back, Jim Bannister pointed out the sign of three riders, possibly a fourth. The sheriff merely nodded and pushed ahead, and his companion followed without comment, though he didn't much like this headlong, blind pursuit.

An ingrained sense of danger was bothering Jim Bannister, turning him apprehensive. He looked at the forward thrust of the lawman's head, the bleak stare, the fingers of ridged muscle lying along his jaw. Sid Parrott had the tenacity of a bulldog, and yet he could be diverted, too—just as now, in his concern about his deputy, he seemed to forget that the man riding beside him was very likely the murderer he had come looking for. Right now he was concerned with working out the trail, that was giving trouble as it led into timber and threatened to lose itself in the thick forest litter. Bannister let him search.

Then the sheriff found it, and they were on their way again. Another stretch of time, then the trees fell back, and they climbed through rocks and brush, crossing a low ridge and quartering down the slope beyond. And suddenly Bannister heard his companion's muttered warning.

Past a rainswollen and sparkling trickle of water, the ground rose again; and there on the open hillside a man sat crosslegged atop a boulder in the sun, with a rifle across his knees. It was the hatchet-faced man Bannister had traded shots with earlier. A cigarette dropped in one corner of his thin-lipped mouth; black eyes watched the riders' approach without any hint of expression, though the rifle's muzzle moved slightly and its bore swung to rest full upon the newcomers.

Nearby, Hack Foley stood with the point of one thick shoulder leaning indolently against a pine trunk. As Bannister and the sheriff reached the flashing trickle of water, which their horses could have taken with a single step, Hack straightened quickly and dropped a hand to his holstered six-shooter. His voice carried above the brawling music of the creek.

"All right! That's far enough!"

CHAPTER VIII

Sid Parrott reined in with his bronc's forelegs almost in the water. Bannister, pulling up beside him, checked his borrowed horse as it tried to get rein length so it could drink. His face still smarted faintly where Hack Foley's nails had clawed it; but, looking at the big man, he could see considerably more signs of the fight, in a badly swollen lip and a discolored cheekbone. Pure hatred stared at him from the piggish little eyes, lighted now with recognition.

"Yes, Hack," Bannister said. "We meet again. You want to take another whack at me?"

The big man lifted his sixgun clear of the leather. "Either of you try crossing that crick," he answered, "and you'll take a slug through the guts!"

Sid Parrott stiffened. He stabbed one broad thumb at the star pinned to his horsehide vest and said angrily, "You Foleys see this?"

The dark-faced man—Bannister had him pegged already as Jed Foley—plucked the quirly from his mouth with his left hand, while the right held its position on the rifle. "Badge or not," he said coldly, "you're on Foley land, Sheriff. Unless you're carrying a warrant for one of us, or for one of our men, get off!"

"I need no warrant!" the sheriff retorted angrily. "I've got a deputy lying hurt in that raid. Maybe hurt bad enough to die."

Jed Foley had a pull at his cigarette, then spoke around the blue drift of smoke from his lips. "We don't know anything about a raid."

"Sure!" big Hack said, with false indignation. "What the hell you trying to pull on us?"

Parrott shook his head. "It won't work. One of you Foleys got licked in a fight, and to even the score you went and ran off that collection herd of Spur cattle. Unlucky for you that you didn't look first and find out there were lawmen visiting the Jackman camp."

Calmly, Jed Foley said, "Let's see you prove some of this."

"Here's the man who gave you a chase and traded lead with you."

They looked at Bannister. Somehow worse than big Hack's naked hatred was the coldly unemotional stare of his brother, as Jed Foley stubbed his smoke against the rock. "He's a liar."

Stung to anger, Bannister lifted his head with a jerk, and his hand made an unthought move toward his gun. At once, Jed Foley was on his feet, crouching, the rifle cradled and ready. "Don't try it!" he warned. To Parrott he added, "You've got no case, Sheriff. Now, both of you get off our range!"

There was a silence so profound, then, that the tiny tinkling of water over stone seemed suddenly very loud. Behind the two Foleys, a pair of waiting horses stirred at their tethers. Bannister's native sense of danger had never spoken so urgently; it led his glance to roam restlessly across the timbered face of the hill before him. And thus it was that he got a fleeting glimpse of sun-reflected brightness.

It was gone before he could quite get his eyes on it, but he knew it for what it was—almost as though someone had raised a shout of warning. A gun barrel. . . .

A glance at Sid Parrott convinced him his companion hadn't noticed. The sheriff still believed they were facing only two opponents. Sweat broke on Bannister as he realized that, if it came to a showdown, the brunt of the thing would lie with him. It would be up to him to take out the lurker on the hill, while at the same time he could expect that Hack Foley would be concentrating all his fury on the one who had beaten and humiliated him.

Carefully he plotted his moves. First shot for the ambush rifle; pray that Hack's initial try would miss! Yet even as his thoughts were busy, Bannister heard himself saying, "It's up to you, Sheriff. I don't like being called a liar, and I don't like having my saddle shot to pieces under me. If you want to try this, I'm ready to back you."

The scene waited on Sid Parrott, then. The silence ran out and the horses moved and stamped restlessly as he looked at the rifle leveled in Jed Foley's grasp, at Hack Foley and the sixshooter in his big hand. Any man would hesitate to draw against such odds, and to one of such native caution as Sid Parrott it was clearly out of the question. He passed a palm across his mouth, pulling it out of shape, and when he dropped the hand a corner of his mouth jerked as though with a nervous tic.

"You damned Foleys!" he exclaimed hoarsely. "You always stack the cards! No one else ever has a chance, the way you play them!"

Jed Foley's thin lips split in a grin that showed the gleam of white teeth. "That's how it is, Sheriff. Either make your move—or drift!"

Parrott's shoulders settled; moving slowly, like an old and very tired man, he picked up the reins and signaled Bannister with a brief glance. Bannister let the lawman go first. As he followed back across the hill the way they had come, he rode half twisted in the saddle, his right hand free, his whole attention on the Foleys as long as they were in sight.

When he caught up with the sheriff, Sid Parrott showed him a look of angry humiliation. He said gruffly, "Thanks for offering to help back there. I suppose you think I should have braved up to them."

"I was hoping you wouldn't," Bannister admitted. "I wasn't sure whether you knew about the third one or not."

"Third one?" the sheriff pulled rein sharply, turned to stare.

Bannister nodded. "He was staked out in the brush on the hill. The sun flashed off his gun barrel. I was afraid you didn't see it, and I couldn't think of a way to warn you."

The lawman breathed in slowly, then blew out his cheeks. There was a faint shine of sweat breaking across them. "I might have guessed," he said finally. "They'd never play it any way but safe." He shook his head. "Damn them!"

"One thing I don't quite understand," Bannister said, looking at him closely, "is how you could stand by and let good people like the Jackmans take on such a proposition as bucking those Foleys."

"I wouldn't have, if I'd known in time. I only met them once, that first day in town. I didn't hear until too late that they were making a deal with Sam Murdock." His eyes narrowed, the wrinkles lying in deep folds at their corners as he looked at his companion. "You know, it's a funny thing, but I keep wondering why we never met, that day in Downey. It ain't such a big town."

Jim Bannister refused to allow any change in his expression. "I suppose I just somehow missed running into you."

"That'd be kind of hard to do, in a place that size," the sheriff said; but even if he were still skeptical, he let the matter drop. And Bannister changed the subject.

"About the Foleys. They may be tough, but it strikes me as odd that they could have the law, and a whole range, this badly buffaloed."

It wasn't a politic thing to say, in the light of Parrott's thinly veiled suspicions; but he was angry. He saw his words spur the sheriff's anger in turn—saw the wrinkled cheeks go taut and smooth and mottled as the color flowed into them and then ebbed again. Sid Parrott's fist became a hard knot, resting on the pommel of his saddle.

"Now you listen to me, Ward! In the eyes of the law, to put it bluntly, your friends ain't much better than interlopers themselves, with Sam Murdock dead. And the one they got to thank for *that* state of affairs is this murderer—this Jim Bannister!"

He all but spat the name, his slate-gray eyes pinned on the other's. And Bannister thought: Go ahead, damn you! If you think I'm your man, why don't you come right out and say it?

But then the other's stare altered and became empty of feeling. The sheriff straightened, lifting the reins. "What I do about the Foleys is no longer their concern—or yours, either. I'm a man who takes one step at a time; and right now my first concern is for my deputy. Bert Grinstead may be dying—or already dead, for all I know. Until I've eased my mind about him, the Foleys will have to wait." With that he roweled his dun horse, and Bannister had no choice but to follow.

Arriving once more at the roundup camp, they found the Jackmans had been doing what they could for Bert Grinstead. His left leg had been set, and splinted with lengths of green timber—a crude but effective job. But he was still unconscious.

Noah had come in shortly before and learned about the raid. Since there was hardly any use trying to gather the stampeded cattle until they knew where they stood legally in relation to Spur, the Jackmans were at work now sorting through the wreckage of their stuff, salvaging whatever was still usable. They moved about the task with the stunned and wooden manner of people who had withstood too many shocks. Even Tansy's remarkable spirits seemed dampened. She straightened slowly and pushed the hair back from her forehead, as she watched Bannister and the sheriff riding out of the draw.

Sid Parrott, brushing aside all questions, dismounted and went directly to look at his hurt deputy; so the Jackmans turned to Bannister and listened while he told them, briefly, of the encounter with the Foleys. No one seemed surprised; no one commented. Their beaten lack of spirit was a sad thing to see.

The sheriff got to his feet after examining Grinstead. "You did a good job on him," he said gruffly. "But I'm worried he don't show any signs of coming out of it. There's a lump on the back of his head I don't like. One kick of a steer's hoof could crack a man's skull like it was an egg."

"You better bring him down to Spur," Uncle El suggested. "The place was a mess when we took over, but we've got things pretty well cleaned up now. We can at least fix him a bed, and we'll do the best we can for him."

The lawman shook his head. "Bert needs a doctor, the sooner the better. Only thing I can see is to get him back to town."

"How do you figure to do it?" Jim Bannister demanded.

For answer, Parrott looked toward the Jackmans' roundup wagon. An ancient spring wagon, without a top, it had been slewed around in the stampede and tilted over on a cramped wheel, but it didn't look as though it was damaged. "If that will roll, maybe I can borrow it."

The Jackmans exchanged a look. Noah said, "We rode that thing all the way down from Wyoming. It ain't much for comfort; it'll jounce a sick man to hell and gone, on these roads."

"It'll have to serve. I can take it slow." Then

Sid Parrott's eyes sought Bannister's; their opaque depths held a sudden spark of thought, but his tone was without expression as he added: "Maybe Jim Ward, here, would oblige by doing the driving. Then I could ride after and see to it that Bert doesn't come to any grief."

Bannister hesitated, feeling a sharp pang of alarm. He saw the trap, and yet the sheriff left him no real ground for refusing. And it would be better, after all, if there must be a showdown, not to have it here, in the presence of these people. Lord only knew, they had troubles enough of their own! "Why—sure," he said, with an effort at casualness, while Parrott's gray stare continued to rest on him, and the Jackmans listened in silence. "That should be all right, I guess."

"Good!" The sheriff seemed determined to snap him up on it before he could think of an excuse to withdraw. "Let's get the wagon ready."

It was fairly rickety, but would serve. They got it straightened out and Bannister laid down a comfortable bed of pine boughs, covering them with what was left of one of the Jackmans' tarps. He helped Parrott lift the unconscious man inside, while Noah and Uncle El hitched up the wagon team. The sheriff tied the deputy's horse to the tailgate, then stepped into the saddle of his big dun.

Noah Jackman came to him, then, hesitating over something he wanted to say. Finally he swallowed and got it out. "Sheriff, I'll be glad to drive the wagon for you."

Taken off guard, Parrott could only blink. "Huh?"

"I said, I'd handle the wagon. If it's all the same to you."

The sheriff fixed him with a shrewd look. Parrott had quickly recovered from his first surprise. It was plain that he saw, now, what the fellow was up to. But Parrott was not to be diverted so easily. He said, blandly but still with a firmness that didn't invite argument, "Why, that's all been settled. Ward said he'd do it."

It had been a gallant try. Bannister could only stare at Noah Jackman, remembering the man's suspicious jealousy and wondering what could have moved him. Even though it hadn't worked, he was pleased and grateful, and he thanked the man with a nod. He could have told him it wouldn't work. . . .

Bannister put a boot on the front wheel hub and stepped to the wagon seat. He settled his big frame there, gathered the reins, kicked off the brake. "Take care of the sorrel till I get back," he called down. "He's got a front leg he's been favoring."

"Sure," Uncle El told him. Bannister yelled at the horses and swung them in a tight circle.

The old wagon groaned in all its timbers and the near front wheel wobbled badly; Bannister found himself wondering how it had ever rought these people all the way from Wyoming. But even when a rear wheel slipped off a half-buried hump of rock, and the wagon box slammed against the bolster, there was no sound at all from the hurt deputy.

CHAPTER IX

As Jed and Hack Foley stood watching the pair of horsemen move out of sight, Mitch Dekin came down from his hiding place on the hill, leading his horse and carrying his rifle by the balance. "Where'd the sheriff come from?" he demanded. "And that big fellow with him, wasn't he the same one that—"

"Yeah, he was the one!" Hack Foley cut in angrily, and touched his lip that was swollen from the punishing weight of the blond stranger's fists. His whole jaw ached yet, and it shortened his temper. "The bastard!" he gritted. "I should have plugged him while I had the chance!"

"Shut up!" his brother said shortly. "Just remember, after this—you *can* be licked." He turned to Mitch, then, with an order. "Get after that pair. Stay out of sight, but find out what they're up to." Mitch, who was good at this sort of assignment, nodded as he turned to his horse. He scrambled to its back and sent it leaping across the rivulet, rifle laid across his knees. Watching him go, Jed Foley told his brother, "This is a damned bad business! You picked a great time to get tough with those people."

Hack scowled darkly. "Wasn't my fault! How'd

I know the sheriff would pick today to show up on this side of the pass?"

"You realize that if that deputy dies on his hands, it's a murder charge."

The big fellow tried to scoff. "Sid Parrott wouldn't have the spine to push it!" But his bluster fell flat. He caught the infection of his brother's somber mood and turned silently to mount, as Jed slid his rifle into the boot of his own saddle and swung astride.

Jed was thinking. At last he said, "We'd best play careful; we may not have heard the last of this. We're holding about fifty head of Long Bars just now. Anything smaller we can pass off as strays; but those Long Bars have got to be pushed out of sight, farther into the hills. Then we'll set the boys to work, have them finish venting the brands, fast, so we can move them out and be rid of them. We better get right at it."

Foley headquarters had never known the civilizing touch of a woman's hand, except once for a period of something less than a week; that time, a couple of girls from Cabra Springs had been inveigled up here to try it, but had got fed up and run off in the middle of the night. They'd been game enough, but the insatiable Hack Foley had turned out to be a little more than they bargained for.

All in all, the place was a good setting for the dozen-odd men who lived there. The fences were usually kept in some repair, out of necessity. The buildings, though, had a patchy and makeshift air about them. They were made of logs, mud chinked, with steep shake roofs to shed the winter snows. The main house had a covered dog run separating bunkroom and kitchen; in these two rooms the Foley brothers lived together with their crew, in a general indiscriminate scramble that the girls from Cabra Springs had found most discouraging.

The slapdash style of living was exemplified by a scatter of rusting tin cans, forming a half circle about the kitchen door at roughly the limit of a man's throwing arm. Shakes missing from the roofs, and broken windowpanes temporarily plugged with rags, would probably have to wait until the advent of winter made it impossible to put off any longer doing something about them.

At sunset, Jed and Hack Foley rode into head-quarters in a bad mood, even though Mitch Dekin had been able to report seeing the Jackmans abandon their roundup camp and trail back to Spur, looking like people who had given up. Mitch had watched as Sid Parrott pulled out with Jackman's wagon, with his hurt deputy in back—still unconscious, but seemingly not dead yet—and the blond stranger handling the team. They were headed toward the pass, so it looked as if there would be a breathing space, at least— time for the crew to finish venting the brands on those Long Bars and dispose of them. So much to the good.

But Jed Foley, stripping gear from his horse at the corral, had a sour look on him. "I'm getting fed up with this setup. We live like pigs!"

"Oh, it ain't so bad," Hack grunted as he tugged at a stubborn cinch strap. "People leave us alone."

"Up to now, maybe. After today, I ain't so sure. . . . And what the hell good do we do ourselves, anyway? How much will we get from them fifty Long Bars? You know how it works: We run the risk, the fence takes the profits. If I just knew a way to lay hands on a piece of real money for once!"

"Well, there's always a bank. And trains." They started toward the house, where lamplight gleamed at them, and woodsmoke from the kitchen chimney laced the early dusk. "That what you mean?"

"With the crew we got?" Jed snorted. "Just barely brains enough, among the lot of them, to dab a rope on a steer and heat a branding iron! What I'd like is to clean out the lot and start from scratch; get some fresh blood in here."

"Yeah? You're always tellin' me how dumb I am!" Hack said, in quick suspicion. "Maybe you'd like to try gettin' rid of *me?*"

Jed shot him a sour look but didn't bother to answer. By now they were at the house, and Morgan, the third brother, eased out through the lighted kitchen doorway and put his shoulders against the edge of it.

He was an in-between sort, this Morgan Foley—not as smart as Jed, or as big as Hack—but his broad-cheeked face was the nearest to handsome of any of the three. He knew this, and was inordinately vain of the ornate mustache he had copied from a bartender he'd seen once, in the biggest saloon in Denver. Lounging in the doorway, he touched the ends of the mustache with the thumb and forefinger of one hand. He said, "You're late enough. Where the hell you been?"

Jed explained; they stood and talked the situation over. Morgan Foley had been off on some business of his own all day, and this was the first he'd known of Hack's trouble with the big stranger, or the raid on the Jackman camp and what followed. He stroked his mustache and heard his brothers out in silence, looking intelligent. "Funny thing," he said then. "I got a kid inside. Picked him up this afternoon in the hills."

Puzzled, Jed frowned at him. "A kid? What kid?"

"Nobody I ever seen—and I reckon we know all the outfits around here. He says his name is Clay Evans. He tried to bolt when he first seen me, and I had to pull a gun to make him quiet down and answer questions. Even then he wouldn't give me answers I liked. So I decided to bring him in."

Hack said, in a tone sharp with sudden interest, "What's this kid look like?"

"Black-headed little hellion, wild as I ever see. He even tried to jump me once, when my back was turned. But I got him pretty well tamed, at the moment." He indicated the kitchen behind him, with a thumb. Hack shoved past and strode heavily inside, the other two following.

The kid sat hunch-shouldered at the big slab table that filled most of the kitchen's crowded space, his elbows on the wood and a tin cup of coffee steaming in front of him. The big wood range pushed heat into the room; an oil lamp in a wall bracket laid its yellow glow over its make-shift furnishings, and deepened the hollows of the strange youngster's brooding face as he peered at the men in the doorway.

"You!" big Hack Foley said. Without breaking stride he tramped into the room, laid a hand on the kid's shoulder, and lifted him bodily to his feet. An openhanded swing of the huge right palm took the kid on the side of the head and flung him, reeling, into the logs of the wall behind him. A metal pan was jarred off a shelf and went clanging to the floorboards.

"What the hell?" Morgan Foley exclaimed.

Hack showed his brother a look of twisted fury. "Damn it, this is the one!" He stabbed a thick

106

pointing finger. "He was there today. He was with the big guy when they jumped me!"

The kid lifted his head with a defiant look. The whole side of his face was a fiery red where the flat of Hack's massive palm had struck. "*I* never jumped you!" he exclaimed hoarsely. "Why take it out on me, just because you wasn't tough enough?"

Hack roared and was after him again, collaring him when he pushed himself away from the wall. At his touch the kid seemed to turn into a wild animal, fighting back with surprising ferocity. A fist caught Hack on his swollen lip; he gave a grunt and swatted the boy, cuffing him the way a bear cuffs a cub, and sending him sprawling against the table. The china cup overturned and went rolling, and coffee spread in a brown tide across the tabletop and cascaded over the edge. Clay Evans caught himself and leaned all his weight on the table, arms atremble and head hanging, dazed from the blow.

Jed Foley said sharply, "Cut it out! Let him alone." He was quicker than his brother; as Hack moved forward again he stepped between and his shoulder struck the big fellow's chest solidly, bringing him up hard. "That's plenty of that!" he snapped and, though Hack could easily have brushed him aside, he made no move to do it. "I kind of like the kid," Jed announced. "I like his spit."

"This punk?" Hack's swollen mouth twisted into a hard sneer. "He's what you mean by new blood, maybe?"

"I might do worse!"

"Hell! Maybe you forgot—he pals around with lawmen!"

The kid was rubbing the side of his head. He stopped, blinking. "What lawmen?" he echoed. As he saw how big Hack put up a hand to finger his bruised cheek, his eyes widened. "You don't mean the guy that beat you up! Him a lawman? Jim Bannister?" He threw back his head and laughed out loud, but the laugh faded as he saw Jed Foley's expression.

"Bannister!"

A sudden quiet descended. "The name mean something to you?" Morgan demanded, looking at his brother.

"Don't tell me you've forgotten the guy that trailed a syndicate man half across New Mexico, a year or so back—ran him to earth in a hotel room, and killed him there. . . . He was tried and marked for a hanging, but he broke out before they had time to stretch him."

"Wait, now!" Morgan fingered his mustache; his brows bunched in thought. "Seems like they're still looking for him, ain't they? With a big reward on him?"

"A whopper!"

Hack Foley had been listening impatiently. He

made a slicing gesture with one huge paw. "It ain't the same one and you know it! You saw this guy riding with the sheriff. It's my opinion they sent the kid to spy on us."

They looked again at the boy. He stood against the rough logs, his face pale and haggard looking in the downward glow of the wall lamp, the lank black hair plastered to his forehead. His eyes showed fear. He shook his head. "That ain't true!" he stammered. "I'm no spy! And the big fellow's no more a lawman than you are. He's Jim Bannister, I tell you!"

The brothers exchanged a look. "Why, sure, kid!" Jed Foley said then. "Take it easy; nobody's gonna hurt you any. Hack, clean up this mess you made." He indicated the spilled coffee, still dripping off the edge of the table. To Morgan he added, "Let's have some more coffee here. And some grub."

The others knew the voice of authority. They moved to carry out orders, puzzled but ready to wait and see just what Jed, the brainy one of the family, had in mind.

"What was your name again?"

Still only half reassured, the young fellow hesitated, wetting his lips. "Clay Evans," he said finally.

"Sit down, Evans," Jed told him, and himself threw a leg across a bench and dropped his elbows on the table. "We'll all sit." He thumbed back his flat-topped sodbuster, gave the kid a friendly surveyal. "Need a job, Evans? Maybe you'd like workin' for me—for us?"

"Yeah?" The boy threw a suspicious glance around. "Doing what?"

Jed shrugged. "Remains to be seen. Who knows? Maybe we can do each other some good." He took the coffeepot Morgan had set on the table, filled two more china cups, shoved one toward the boy.

"But first, I'm curious," he said. "Suppose you tell me exactly what you know about this fellow Bannister."

CHAPTER X

The sheriff proved to be an unrelenting pace setter. He was too sharply roweled by concern over his hurt deputy to care about anyone else, or even the horses, and Bannister felt enough sympathy with him not to argue. The slow hours dragged on to the creaking of that wobbly wagonwheel, and still Bert Grinstead lay without stirring and without any sign of returning consciousness, only the continued rise and fall of his breathing to show he was alive. His body gave to every lurch of the clumsy vehicle. Bannister tooled it, as carefully as he could, over the outcroppings and around the deeply eroded ruts, but they made it impossible for a wagon with a hurt man in it to maneuver this wretched mountain road at any speed.

Dusk caught them with the pass still ahead, and still Sid Parrott kept pressing on; it seemed apparent that he meant to continue like this, without stopping to make camp. The horses, though, were tiring badly, and as the night deepened it was becoming necessary to stop for longer periods at a time in order to give them a chance to rest. During these delays the sheriff fretted impatiently; but Bannister knew they could ask only so much of the weary team, and each time he refused to move on until he judged they were able.

When at last the pass leveled out, the starry sky was like a bowl of white fires crowding close, broken only where a few rags of cloud still moved across the stars and the face of the moon. The moon dropped from sight as they began their descent, on the far side of the hills.

At some hour late in the night they broke out of the timber and saw the broad roofs and the dark buildings of Murdock's place lying before them.

No lights showed. At an order from the sheriff, Bannister halted his team in the clearing before the silent store buildings. "I'll see if I can rouse Harry Jones," the lawman said as the quiet settled about them. Saddle leather popping, he swung heavily to the ground.

Bannister, not answering, drew his gun and laid it in his lap, a finger in the trigger guard. He had been thinking ahead to this moment, had been able to see no way around it. Harry Jones, of course, could identify him positively as the man he had seen standing under his employer's gun, the one old Murdock had named as Jim Bannister. This would not prove him guilty of killing Murdock, of course. It wouldn't even prove that he actually was Bannister. But it would give the lie to the alibi Tansy Jackman had improvised for him. And it would give the sheriff every excuse to hold him for further investigation.

Well, Bannister thought, he had bluffed this far; he'd continue to play the cards as they fell.

He sat there on the wagon seat, with tiredness draining through him and the hurt deputy lying like a dead man in the box at his back. There was a sound of horses stirring in the pen, yonder. Now he heard the crunch of Sid Parrott's footsteps approaching the dark store building, the hollow thump of the gallery steps beneath his boots. The sheriff called Jones' name, pounded the door and tried to work the latch. When he raised no answer, Parrott descended the steps again and walked away around the side of the building; the night swallowed him.

Minutes later he was back. Dropping a hand on the broad iron tire of a wagonwheel, he said, "No sign of Harry. I understand he was due to deliver some saddle stock for old Murdock, over to Cabra Springs. I suppose that's where he's gone."

Bannister felt a relief so intense he didn't trust himself to speak. He kept silent, and the othe man continued: "Murdock's wagon team is in the pen. There's feed and water available. We'll swap for these beat-out critters of Jackman's and keep going."

"All right," Bannister said roughly, and swung stiffly down to help make the switch.

・ ・ ・

Downey proved to be a mill town, strung out through the timber along a bench where a creek had been dammed to make a shallow log pond. There was the long, shedlike structure housing the big saw, the dark bulk of the steam engine that ran it, the piles of slash for burning, and the stacks of drying boards. A yellow ground cover of sawdust was everywhere, and a pungent pine smell.

Beyond a fringe of shanties that housed the millworkers were the few crooked and uneven streets of the town itself. These had been hacked from the jackpine forest, and were lined by a miscellany of rough one and two story clapboard buildings. Every window was dark as the wagon creaked slowly along the winding main street, the noise it made sounding doubly loud against the sleeping quiet of the village. The air smelled of dawn.

Parrott guided the way around a corner where a narrower side street ran across, and ordered a halt before a low-roofed shack of board-and-batten construction that looked as though it had never known paint. While Bannister waited, the sheriff hurried up a rattling wooden walk to the door. After a moment of pounding he roused a light to life somewhere inside. The door opened, and, after a few words from Sid Parrott, a man came out, carrying an oil lamp in one hand and

114

trying to stuff the tail of a nightgown into his pants at the same time. He brought the lamp and held it to get a look at the injured deputy. His lantern-jawed face, under a wild tangle of thinning white hair, wore a somber look as he reached to thumb open Bert Grinstead's closed eyelids. He shook his head.

"Been unconscious since noon yesterday, you say? I don't like that. It means a concussion, at the very least—always a dangerous proposition."

The sheriff said, "We better help you get him inside."

But the doctor had other ideas. "He's going to need somebody looking after him constantly, and I couldn't promise him that. I get too many calls. I suggest we take him home. It's only a couple of blocks farther, and he'll have his wife to do for him. Why don't you roll him on around there, and I'll skin into some clothes and be right over."

"Whatever you say, Doc," Sid Parrott agreed, and turned again to mount his saddle.

The Grinstead place was a tidy little house with a picket fence and even a few late flowers, that looked black now against the white paint. A hint of gray light was beginning to filter through the night, and overhead the stars showed paler among the tops of the pine trees. Here the hammering of Parrott's fist, against a screen door that rattled to the pounding, again made lamplight glimmer into being somewhere beyond a dark window. The light chased shadows before it as someone carried it through the house while coming to answer the door.

A woman opened to him, a woman in a night-dress and a wrapper, with dark hair done up in a single thick braid that fell across her shoulder and breast. She stared out at Parrott and at the wagon, but the sheriff took her by an elbow and firmly guided her back into the house, relieving her of the lamp as he did so, as though he were afraid she might drop it. For a moment they stood just inside the door, earnestly talking. Then Jim Bannister heard a single, heart-stabbing cry from the woman. The sheriff came back, tramping out to the wagon and telling Bannister, in a voice roughened by feeling: "All right, let's move him in. Goddamn it, what a business!"

By the time they had Bert Grinstead out of the wagon and carried into the house, a place was ready for him in the bed his wife had left to answer the door. The bedroom opened off the living room. She hovered anxiously as they maneuvered the narrow doorway and laid her husband down, fully dressed. The doctor came bustling in at about that time, more or less dressed himself, though he had only shoved his feet into carpet slippers, and had no shirt on under his black alpaca coat. He set a cracked leather bag on the table by the bed, and opened it. Jim

Bannister, feeling unneeded, went out into the living room and let himself onto the edge of a stiff chair beside the front door, his hat on his knees.

It was chilly in there, but all he was aware of really was that he had never been nearer exhaustion. Weariness seemed to drag at him, running from his drooping shoulders down through every limb. It was a moment before he realized he was not alone. Then, at a sound, he looked up and saw a half-dressed youngster of fourteen or so standing with his back to a closed door, solemnly regarding him with eyes that were dark with concern and still dazed by sleep. They stared at one another wordlessly.

From the open bedroom door, snatches of somber talk reached them—the doctor commenting half to himself as he made his examination: "Some-body did a good job of splinting that broken leg . . . looks like a couple of cracked ribs; from his breathing, don't think they've hurt the lung . . . there's the lump on the side of the skull where one of them steers must have tromped him. . . ."

Sid Parrott said anxiously, "What do you think, Doc? Will he pull out of this?"

"We're going to have to wait and see." There was a remark from the woman which Bannister couldn't hear; then the doctor said, "If you two will leave me alone with him, I can get my work done easier. You too, Ruthie."

Parrott and the woman came into the living room and the door closed behind them. In the strengthening, grainy light seeping in from outdoors, Bannister could see that she was a nice-looking person, possibly in her early thirties, to judge by the size of her son. Her home was like her—rather sparsely furnished, as a deputy sheriff's house was apt to be on his salary, but spotless and graced with the rare atmosphere of a real home. Just now she was wringing her hands, slowly and unconsciously.

The sheriff put a hand gently on her shoulder and told her, "You go get some rest now, Ruthie, while you got a chance."

"I couldn't!"

"You'll need it. This is gonna be a long pull, and it's gonna all be on your shoulders. While Doc and me are here, let it slide off on ours for a minute or so, at least." He added, "Would there be any coffee on the stove that Jim and me can heat up?"

For the first time she seemed to see the stranger, who hadn't moved from his chair by the door. She looked at the sheriff and said in self-condemnation, "Why, you both are beat plumb to a frazzle—and all to get Bert home to me! Come in the kitchen and let me fix you some breakfast."

"The coffee will do fine," Parrott insisted, and Jim Bannister, coming to his feet now, agreed.

"I want to wait and get the doc's word, after he's through," the sheriff said. "Then we'll take the wagon and horses around to the livery, and—"

"Howie can take care of that," the woman said. "It's little enough."

She made a gesture to the boy that brought him quickly forward. "Sure. No trouble at all, Sid."

The sheriff acquiesced, with a tired lift of the shoulders and a nod. "Thanks a lot, Howie. Tell George I'll be around later and square it with him." Then, as Howie went hurrying out into the morning, where a few birds were making tentative salutes to the dawn, Sid Parrott looked at Bannister.

"Let's go into the kitchen, Jim," he said, "before I fall asleep where I'm standing."

CHAPTER XI

Jim Bannister came awake gradually, with a bewildered sense of alarm as he tried to determine where he was. He had been sleeping the sleep of exhaustion, his big body cramped and folded somehow into the confines of an ancient horsehair sofa. He was dressed, except for his hat and boots. He got his legs straightened out, dropped his stockinged feet to the floor, and looked around him uncomprehendingly at a room he was sure he had never seen before. It was certainly not Bert Grinstead's living room.

Then he remembered leaving Grinstead's little house, in the first pink flush of sunrise, and walking with Sid Parrott the short block here to the sheriff's own bachelor quarters. No hotel in this town, Parrott had said, but he was welcome to bed down on the sofa. Bannister had never intended to take him up on it, and never intended to fall asleep; but the drained condition of his body betrayed him. Now he saw that the sun was high; it was probably close to noon. A feeling of depression settled on him as he sat and rubbed his hands across his head and over the heavy stubble of yellow whiskers that scratched his palm.

He looked around him. It seemed like the kind

of place Sid Parrott would live in, somehow—not too tidy, dust in the corners, furnishings that looked as though the sheriff had scavenged them when more particular people had thrown them away. The threadbare carpet under his feet had been burned through in a number of places, as though by careless cigarettes. His boots stood nearby; he hauled them over and began to pull them on.

As he did so, he became aware of the smell of cooking and the sound of activity somewhere at the back of the house. He realized he had been aware of them without really noticing them; possibly they were what had wakened him. He got his boots on and stood, stretching the cramps out of his muscles. On the back of a chair he saw his gun and belt hanging. When he took the gun from its holster, and spun the cylinder, he saw it was fully loaded. Bannister strapped the weapon into place and then went hunting the source of those smells of frying bacon and brewing coffee.

In the kitchen, Sid Parrott looked around at him from the rusty wood stove, where he stood turning strips of bacon in a frypan sputtering in grease. He gave his guest a genial nod, told him, "I was beginning to think I'd have to kick you off that sofa. I'll have some grub here in a few minutes. Just getting ready to fry the eggs."

Bannister said, "I can use them."

Eying the stubble of beard shining yellow on

the big man's cheeks, the sheriff jerked his head toward a plank sideboard nailed in the corner of the kitchen. "There's soap and a razor on the shelf yonder."

Bannister felt of his jaw and nodded. "Thanks. I didn't bring mine along."

"Help yourself. Just pour out some hot water from the kettle there."

The sputter of frying eggs filled the kitchen as the sheriff went on with his work. Presently he was whistling tunelessly. Bannister, having made quick work of his shaving, finished toweling his face and took a chair at the table, with its threadbare oilcloth that had been scrubbed clean of its original pattern. He said, "You sound like you're in a good mood."

Parrott slid fried eggs onto a platter, arranged strips of crisp bacon around them. "Dig in." He set a pot of coffee on the table, straddled the chair across from Bannister. As he poured for them both he went on: "I been over to see Bert again while you were still sleeping. There's good news. He's come to, in spite of that knock on the head. Looks like he's going to be all right."

"I'm glad to hear that," Bannister said, and meant it.

The sheriff nodded. "Doc gives him every chance, now. He's just got to take it easy so as to let those bones knit, and make sure there's nothing worse the matter. I've told Bert I don't want to see him around the office for at least a month."

In his great relief at thus settling his fears for Bert Grinstead, the sheriff didn't seem able to quit talking; and Jim Bannister let him talk, while he occupied himself by filling the void in his middle. Hearing Sid Parrott run on, seeing the animation in his expressive and oddly wrinkled features, watching him gesture with an egg-stained knife-blade, Bannister almost hated to bring him down. But it was inevitable, and the words came now as Bannister laid his own silverware on his emptied plate and pushed the plate away. He picked up his coffee mug, drained it off, set it down again.

"Well," he said, "thanks for the meal. I should be able to cover quite a few miles on the strength of that."

He saw the other's face change subtly. The animation cooled in the sheriff's eyes; the lids came down, hooding the stare he put on the bigger man as his mouth settled into a frown. He laid down his knife and said carefully, "You figure to be riding?"

Bannister had dug tobacco from his shirt pocket and was beginning to build a cigarette. "Why, I figure you won't need me now. Thought I'd pick up the Jackmans' wagon at the livery, switch teams again at Murdock's, and head on back across the pass. Any objections?"

He watched the other, across his hands. The sheriff would be a very poor poker player; that face of his gave away every shade of feeling. Just now he faced a real decision. He had used Bert Grinstead's injury to keep this stranger with him and get him down here, across the pass, but the ruse would serve no longer. So far he had not had to challenge Bannister openly as to his identity; he had not had to touch a gun. The moment was very nearly upon him when he would have no other choice. Yet, being a cautious man—and maybe even a little afraid of someone with Jim Bannister's reputation—the sheriff still hesitated to move.

Bannister methodically finished rolling and twisting and tonguing closed the tube of paper and tobacco, waiting. He hated to put pressure on the man. He was beginning to like and respect Sid Parrott.

Putting the cigarette in his mouth, he looked around and located a box of matches on the shelf above the stove. He got up, went and helped himself to several, snapped one alight and fired up. As he peered at the lawman through the blue spurt of smoke, he decided to give Parrott a little more time; and so, shaking out the match and dropping it into the woodbox, he said, "Before I can leave, I got a little business to take care of over in town. This lawyer, the one you said is handling Murdock's estate—I'd like a talk with him, to try and get some idea of just where the

Jackmans stand. Can you tell me where I'd locate him?"

Sid Parrott drew a breath, and Bannister saw him wet his lips with the tip of his tongue. "Sure. He's got an office upstairs over the bank; you can't miss it. It's one of the few two-story buildings."

"Thanks," Bannister said. "I'll go look him up. I'll be there, if you should want anything."

He walked out of the kitchen, found his hat and coat where he had left them on a chair by the front door. He heard the sheriff push back his chair, but Parrott made no move to follow him. He pulled on his hat and walked out into the clear morning, and the town that was dominated by the whine of the sawmill, the coughing of the steam engine, the pungent gray smoke rising from the burning pile of slash.

Jim Bannister had a poor notion of lawyers, based on the greasy, sweating incompetent who had made a fiasco of defending him in his own murder trial, and on the cold and sinisterly smooth legal machines, with the smell of money about them, who had conducted matters on behalf of the syndicate and achieved his conviction with flawless ease. Claude Pine seemed to fall somewhere between the two types: Those Chicago lawyers would have eaten him alive, but behind the scarred desk of a small-town law office he was in his own domain, and he showed his power. A man with the beginning of a paunch, and dark hair receding from the temples of an intelligent, clean-shaven face, he studied Bannister with eyes that were trained to probe and at the same time to contain their own thoughts.

He said, "What was the name again?"

"Ward, Jim Ward. But that's neither here nor there," Bannister insisted. "What I'm concerned about is the folks I work for. They got to know where they stand."

"Yes. . . ." The man spread his hands, laced the fingers together, and put them down on the blotter before him. The hands were white and plump, with dark hairs growing on their backs. "Afraid there's not much I can say to help you. I do recall, now, that Sam Murdock mentioned something to me about having hired the Jackmans to work that Spur cattle for him. As I remember, the deal was for a dollar a head on any they managed to dig out of the timber and deliver to the railroad at Cabra Springs."

"A dollar a head!" Anger tightened Bannister's mouth. "Does that sound reasonable to you? Do you think anyone in his right mind would agree to work for that kind of pay—with the Foleys sure to make a fight of it?"

Pine lifted a shoulder. "The Jackmans were pretty hard up; they might have been in no position to bargain. And nobody ever said Sam

Murdock was the kind to give more than he had to."

"I can believe *that!*" Bannister said grimly. "I can also believe he never told anyone the honest truth unless there was money in it for him."

"Honesty is a word with a good many shades of meaning," Claude Pine commented dryly. "In matters of business it means what's in the small print of the contract. Sam Murdock was a businessman; most people thought of him as an eccentric old storekeeper, but as a matter of fact he owned a good piece of this town and was a silent partner in the sawmill." He nodded toward the window and the whining saw, that one soon became so used to he barely noticed it. "Unless there's a contract, with a signature on it in writing I can identify as Sam's, the Jackmans haven't much of a leg to stand on. I'm sorry." But he spoke coldly, his tone belying the sentiment.

Jim Bannister scowled. He slapped his hat against his knee and came surging up from his chair. He said bitterly, "Murdock must have been a real proud man, knowing the things he put over on other people!"

The lawyer looked up at the tall shape of the yellow-haired stranger. "I'm expecting his sister in on the afternoon stage. She's his only surviving relative, and she'll inherit everything. The Jackmans could talk to her about their problem. That's the best suggestion I can offer."

Bannister returned the look, his eyes hard. "And, as her attorney, what are you going to advise her to do about it?"

"I'm afraid that's not a question I feel free to answer."

"Figured as much." Bannister pulled on his sweated hat. "All right," he said. "Thanks for your time. I'll keep in mind what you've told me." He turned and walked out of the lawyer's office and down the dark well of the enclosed staircase, where his footsteps thundered and echoed as though in a tunnel.

Claude Pine sat for a long minute listening to those footsteps recede, his eyes narrowed and a great excitement growing in him. While the man had sat opposite him he had kept both hands carefully in sight upon the desktop. Now, however, with a resolute movement he pulled open a drawer of the desk, and took out a snubnosed revolver, and slipped it into a side pocket of his suitcoat. Afterward, with one hand on the gun, he got up and went to the window that overlooked the crooked, dusty street.

He looked for the big stranger, but could catch no sight of him, though his glance scoured the street in either direction. Then, as he started to turn away, he saw Sid Parrott angling across the dust toward his office. At once the lawyer hurried to the door and down through the dark stairwell, and met the sheriff on the walk below.

He thought he detected the faintest hint of alarm in the latter's face.

The lawman said, almost too casually, "You didn't happen to see anything of a stranger, did you? Man named Ward. He said he was coming to look you up."

"Yellow-haired giant of a fellow? Claims to work for the Jackman outfit?" The attorney nodded. "He was here. But I'm damned if his name is Ward. Unless I'm completely crazy, he's that Jim Bannister—that killer who did for Sam Murdock!"

Parrott seemed to wince slightly. "I'll admit the thought crossed my mind," he said gruffly. "But what makes you so certain?"

"Two things: First, he fits to a T the man Harry Jones said he saw at the store, the day Sam was killed; and you'll have to admit there don't come many men quite that big! But, even more important, I met those Jackmans when they just hit the country—had quite a long conversation about the possibilities of finding any ranch property hereabouts they could take over. I learned a lot about their affairs, but there was no mention at all of them having brought anyone down from Wyoming with them—named Ward, or anything else!"

A faint sheen of sweat stood on the sheriff's cheeks, though the day was not at all warm. He ran a palm across his face, the soft flesh pulling smoothly beneath his fingers. "I been reading it the same way," he conceded. "But I've been hoping for definite proof, one way or the other. I don't like to move unless I'm sure. After all, if this *is* Bannister, he's going to be a dangerous man to tackle."

Claude Pine took his hand from his pocket, let the other see the gun in it. "I'll back you," he said. "I owned no love to Sam Murdock, but he *was* a client of mine. And if it's a matter of needing help, with twelve thousand on Bannister's head, we should be able to find plenty!"

"I'm not afraid to do my duty," the sheriff said without anger, "once I'm sure where it lies. What I don't want is a manhunt—a lot of amateurs hungry for the reward, and stirring up a hue and cry that can only end in innocent people getting hurt or even killed."

"Agreed," Claude Pine said succinctly. "The two of us, then. But we'd better hurry. You tell me what you want, and I'll do my best to—"

"It's Bannister!"

The shout broke upon them without warning, startling and immobilizing them both. For a moment they could only stand and stare at one another, as they heard the cry being taken up in a dozen throats.

The men of Downey knew that name, of course; they'd been hearing very little else in the two days since Murdock's body was brought in.

Already the street that had been nearly deserted a moment ago was beginning to take on life, as people poured out of the buildings. Up the street, in a pounding flurry of hoofbeats, a rider came spurring and raising the alarm. It was Harry Jones.

Someone ran out to grab for the bridle and shout a question, but he had to leap aside as Sam Murdock's handyman barreled past. Now Jones had caught sight of Parrott and the lawyer, and he came straight at them. Plainly, he was just in off the trail from Cabra Springs; mount and man were both well stained with trail dust. He pulled rein

so abruptly that the pair were spattered with the grit gouged up by iron shoes. "I just seen him, Sheriff!" Jones cried hoarsely. "The fellow Sam was holding under his gun just before he was killed. Big, yellow-haired bastard—I tell you, he's here in this very town right now!"

Sid Parrott drew a long breath, and shared a glance with the lawyer. More doors were banging, more voices taking up a confused shouting. The sheriff sighed. "All right, Harry. Where did you see him? What was he doing?"

"Heading for the livery."

The sheriff pulled his gun. He said heavily, "Looks like I got my work cut out for me, then."

After a few strides he was breaking into a run.

CHAPTER XII

At the first break of sound, a sure instinct for such things told Jim Bannister the situation. He hadn't known he was discovered, but he moved on the instant, stepping close to the crooked line of buildings and putting his broad shoulders against sunwarped clapboard while he shot a hurried, assessing glance in both directions along the street.

He saw a clot of men forming, saw dust swirling around a mounted figure that looked rather like the handyman, Harry Jones. That explained everything.

Bannister heard his own name being repeated by a dozen hoarsely shouting voices. He cursed silently, and drew back into the narrow opening between a pair of buildings. No chance now of reaching the livery barn, and he saw no tied horses anywhere within reach. Doors were slamming; he could hear aimless running feet and a steadily rising hubbub. Suddenly there was even the beginning clamor of an iron bar striking the tire iron that apparently served the town for a fire alarm.

Someone went running past the mouth of the passageway where he stood. They hadn't found him yet, but it would not take long, once the manhunt got under way.

132

He turned and faded quickly back through the slot between the buildings. Beyond lay a straggling, weed-grown alley, and then a scatter of shacks—mere hovels, occupied by the itinerant families of the sawmill hands. With the clangor of the tire iron to spur him on, Bannister kept going. He crossed the alley, ran through a barren yard where dingy laundry flapped on a line. Then he fell into one of a number of footpaths that made a fan converging on the creek bank where the mill stood.

A carpet of yellow sawdust muffled his footsteps. Stacks of green lumber rose about him like the walls of a maze. He broke out of that and the mill itself was before him, and the log pond filled with big red sticks awaiting the saw.

Rumor of the chase had as yet failed to reach this far; the clang of the tire iron was buried under the chuffing of the steam engine, the screech of the big saw, the sharp wine of a smaller saw that a millhand was using to buck lengths of firewood for the boiler. Nearby, a huge pile of waste was burning, throwing off heat and black billowing smoke, with bright flames at its heart. The heat and pungent smell of the burning washed against him as he went past. Several men stopped work to stare at him, and one shouted something, but he didn't pause.

He reached the log pond, hesitated briefly, then turned along it toward the dam of rock and mud and logs that closed off the downstream end and caused the water to back up. He ran out on this and, halfway across, heard a sound that made him pause for a look back, beginning to breathe a little heavily now. The manhunt had discovered him; the big saw had fallen silent, its racket replaced by a growing chorus of shouting voices as men poured blackly down toward the shore of the pond. Bannister saw pointing arms flung in his direction, saw the glint of sunlight on gun barrels.

His mouth grim, he slipped out his own belt gun and flung a couple of bullets into the air above the heads of those on the bank. Sounds of the shots echoed across the water, were sopped up by the thick jackpine timber all around. The men broke and scattered, though the bullets had not even come close to them. One or two who had ventured to set foot on the end of the narrow dam scrambled hastily back, stumbling over one another and narrowly avoiding ending up in the water.

Deliberately, Bannister stood and kicked the spent shells from his revolver, then replaced them as he waited to see what the men yonder would do. As a generality, he knew, men had no real stomach for danger, though the lure of reward money and the mindless excitement of the mob might sweep them on. Already some were running along the bank, trying to find another way across. Jim Bannister rolled the cylinder shut, gave it a spin against the flat of his palm, then turned and sprinted on across the dam.

The wall of jackpine stood before him. He lunged between the narrow, close-standing trunks and at once was swallowed up by shadow. He kept going, dodging brush and leaping down-timber. Finally, in a hollow where fallen trees made a jackstraw tangle, he took cover and waited to regain his breath and to listen for pursuit.

He could hear nothing at first except the laboring of his own lungs, and the normal forest sounds. But as he got his breathing under control and was about to plunge ahead, he began to hear other noises that sent him quickly deeper into hiding.

Behind him, branches were snapping and dry brush cracking from the inexpert blundering of many bodies. Now voices were calling back and forth, faint and confused sounds. Once a gun went off, as someone evidently loosed a shot at some supposed movement in the tangled brush.

Bannister crouched deep into his hiding place, choking on dust and with the sweat running off him. Through interlacing branches he caught glimpses of movement as men went beating through the timber, almost within his reach; it seemed for moments as though the swelling racket of crackling limbs and trampling boots would engulf him. But then, slowly, the sounds faded. The hunters had passed within yards, and gone on.

He came to his feet, easing cramped joints and aching muscles. He rubbed a palm through the sweat and dirt on his cheeks and listened, but there was no evidence that the search would swing back and discover him. At last, carefully, and as silently as he could manage, Bannister moved ahead.

Some time later the trees fell away, and there was an open slant of slick granite before him, with more trees—big yellow-boled pines—standing beyond it. He studied this for long minutes, hesitant about leaving cover and exposing himself. But there was no turning back; that way lay the town, no good to him except for the slim chance of getting his hands on a horse. He was afoot, and likely to stay that way—afoot, and dirty and scratched and torn from his precipitous flight through the scrub timber.

Now he watched the treetops, but there was no circling of disturbed camprobbers, nothing to indicate that his pursuers were in the neighborhood. He moved out of the trees finally and dropped on down the slant, sliding on his bootheels and making the last few yards in running leaps. At the bottom he put his back to a red treetrunk and looked across at the timber he had just left.

High in a cloud-dotted sky a lone hawk swung and circled lazily on scimitar wings, but that was all. So much to the good. Jim Bannister pushed away from the rough bark, turning—and brought up to stare at the trio of riders who sat their horses without movement, eying him. Jed Foley said pleasantly, "Howdy, Bannister."

He looked from one to another of them, feeling a heavy and hopeless residue settle inside him. Jed and Hack he already knew, of course; from the family resemblance the third man, with the mustache, would have to be the third Foley brother—Morgan, he remembered hearing Tansy Jackman name him. All three had guns in their hands, carelessly but suggestively pointed in his direction. To reach his own holster, he knew with sure fatality, would be a bootless mistake. So he stood loose, his hands at his sides, and tried not to let them see the high tension in him.

He said, "Where the devil did you come from?"

Hack Foley showed his teeth in a crooked grin of pure pleasure. "Why, now, we was up yonder. On the ridge." He jerked a splayed thumb across a shoulder. "You get a fine view. We could see all the excitement—them fellers combin' the timber, and you on the run ahead of 'em. Looked real funny from up there. Just like a passel of fleas combin' through the hide of a mangy hound dog." He laughed, a breathy whinny of sound.

"We-uns could see you'd throw 'em off," Jed Foley added. "Figured you'd be coming out of the timber somewhere about here, so we rode down. You come right to us."

"So I see." Bannister lifted his shoulders and let them fall. His right hand brushed a trifle too close to the gun in his holster, and at once Jed Foley's weapon moved slightly, dropping more directly into line. Bannister said, "You used a name just now. . . ."

"It was your own," Jed answered flatly. "Don't try to make out different and get us confused. We found out all about you, mister. Your name's Jim Bannister, and there's a big chunk of money riding on you."

"And where'd you hear this?"

"That's our business." Jed lifted a leg across the cantle of his saddle, swung down. He gestured with the gun barrel. "Now, let's suppose you unhook that shellbelt and dump the whole works, right there at your feet. Don't feel tempted to try anything."

Not arguing any longer, Bannister moved his hands to the belt buckle and began working the tongue of leather through it. To offer resistance was foolishly chancy; still, survival for him had long since become a matter of taking risks. Imperceptibly he was altering the balance of his weight upon his boots, gauging the distance toward the meager shelter of the nearest thick-trunked pine.

He made his move, at the same moment giving the loosened belt a yank that jerked the loaded holster directly into his hand. He heard a yell of alarm as the butt of the holstered gun struck his palm and his fingers closed on it, grabbing it free. Then bootleather slipped on slick rock underfoot; he went heavily to one knee. The ground shook as a horse lunged toward him. And before he could regain his footing, big Hack Foley launched himself from the saddle and bore him down.

The gun was trapped under him and Bannister fought to free it. By now, however, they were all on him—sweating, cursing men who swarmed over him and effectively trapped his arms. A boot toe struck his wrist, sent the gun spinning. He found himself dragged to his feet, and Hack Foley's ugly face was shoved into his own; spittle struck his cheek as the big fellow yelled hoarsely, "Here's a little something for yesterday, bucko!"

Bannister saw the gun barrel descending and tried desperately to roll with the blow as it descended. But his enemies held him helpless and it struck, solidly. His head seemed fairly to explode; his knees broke under him. There was a second blow but he never felt it, nor did he know when they let him sag senseless to the ground.

CHAPTER XIII

He lay where he had been dumped onto a hard bunk, his face pressing into stale-smelling blankets that reeked faintly of sweat and whiskey. Earlier there had been intermittent awareness of a saddle, with himself lashed belly down across it and swaying helplessly to the lurch of the horse moving under him. How long that had gone on, he could only dimly guess.

He had been there, now, for some time, unable and unwilling to move. Past the splitting ache in his skull he was aware of a tumble of voices, and of words that made only occasional sense to him. But presently he was able to concentrate on the voices. Among the others he recognized Jed Foley's, and big Hack's coarse, high-pitched laugh. At last, feeling he would suffocate if he didn't get his face out of the blanket, he worked a hand under him and pushed against it, and levered himself over onto one side.

At once the voices stopped. Through the glow of a kerosene lamp, Jim Bannister peered around. The room was log-walled and lined with crude double-tiered wooden bunks covered with straw mattresses. That smell of sweat and stale whiskey was everywhere. He had been thrown, fully dressed, onto one of the bottom bunks, near a rusty-bellied stove that sent waves of heat into the space around it. At a deal table that held tin cups, plates, and a jug of whiskey three men sat staring at him. They were the Foleys, all of them.

A fourth man, whose face Bannister couldn't see, was slumped on another of the lower bunks, while a fifth lay stretched comfortably on the one over him. The skinny fellow named Mitch stood with one elbow leaning on the wooden frame, talking idly. Now, as Jim Bannister pushed himself undecidedly to a sitting position, Mitch turned and snatched up a shotgun, letting its muzzle fall quickly into line on the prisoner. His eyes gleamed dangerously.

There was danger everywhere Bannister looked.

No question in his mind where he was: This would be the Foley spread. He was back again across the pass, back into the deep hills. Dark night pressed against the window yonder; he must have been laid out for hours, long enough for them to bring him all the way up here from Downey. Unarmed, he was helpless.

He put up a hand, shakily, ran stiff fingers through his hair. Toward the back of his scalp he found a place so tender that he winced and nearly blacked out again. There was a high, spiteful burst of laughter from Hack Foley's barrel chest.

"Finally comin' out from that little tap on the

skull, I guess. You'd think we-uns had hurt him!"

Bannister looked at the man silently. He thought it was his own gun and belt he could see, strapped around the big fellow's middle. And then, past Hack's thick shoulder, he saw the man who sat on that other bunk lift his head. For the first time Bannister got a look at his face.

It was Clay Evans.

There was guilt in the young fellow's eyes, and a sullen defiance that melted before Bannister's answering stare. His mouth worked and his glance wavered and then drifted away, unable to hold steady. He left Bannister with a sick sense of uncleanness and betrayal. There was now, at least, no question as to how the Foleys had managed to learn who he was.

At the table, Jed Foley grunted something that must have been an order, because Mitch Dekin grumbled and, putting down his shotgun, turned and walked out through the door at one end of the room. A gust of cold air swirled in and the flame wavered in the throat of the lamp chimney. Jed picked up the whiskey jug and poured amber liquid into a tin cup, shoved the cup across the tabletop in Bannister's direction.

"Have a slug."

Bannister considered and shook his head. Whatever was in the jug, he doubted if he could handle it just yet. Jed shrugged, and his brother

142

Hack reached and snagged the cup for himself. He drained off a good part of it, wiped the ball of a thumb across his mouth.

"If you'd been willing to act reasonable," Jed Foley said pleasantly, "we wouldn't of had to rough you up."

"Surprises me you didn't kill me and have done with it," Bannister retorted. "Or didn't he tell you the reward's payable either way?" He stabbed Clay with an accusing glance as he spoke, and the boy dropped his eyes to the hands that lay knotted in his lap.

"Oh, we knew," Jed assured him. "But you give us a little problem. Until we solve it, there's not much choice but to keep you alive."

He didn't take the trouble to explain just then. Mitch was back with a plate of food steaming in his hands. He dropped it without ceremony into Bannister's lap. There were beans and a chunk of pork, and a thick slab of bread sitting on top. Bannister looked at the food for a moment, uncertainly; then he decided he had better try to get it down, and picked up the fork.

He was still sick from the blows of the gun barrel. At the first mouthful of food he was seized with acute nausea and had to clamp his throat muscles against it. He got down a good swallow of the beans, and that helped somewhat. Tearing off a chunk of bread, Bannister commenced eating with stolid determination.

His captors watched, almost amiably. He might have been a stray animal one of the boys had picked up and brought home. Jed Foley, lounging at the table, pursued the line of his previous conversation. "Yeah, now that we got you, there's some little question in our minds just what we're going to do with you. We don't want to kill you; the syndicate can do that for us, and pay us too. On the face of it, shouldn't be no trick at all cashing you in for that twelve grand the syndicate offers; but maybe it ain't so simple, when you come right down to it. I don't trust Sid Parrott; he might want a share of the reward."

"Tough," Bannister said curtly. "My heart bleeds for you."

He was having his own troubles. The room was starting to spin around him, slowly, and grainy blackness was pulsing through the lamplight to the beat of his own throbbing head. Suddenly the nausea had returned, tightening his throat convulsively, and he was forced to put a forkful of beans back onto the plate untouched.

If that gun barrel across the skull could do all this to him, he supposed it most likely meant a concussion. That made him think of the deputy, Bert Grinstead, and the way he had looked lying between life and death. The thought was enough to start a cold sweat breaking all over his body.

Hack Foley's voice came as though from some considerable distance: "Thing looks simple enough to me. I don't trust that bastard Sid Parrott any more'n the rest of you do. But there's other sheriffs and other law offices where we can turn him in and put in our claim. And if he gives us any trouble before we get him there, there's nothin' to stop us from plugging him."

Bannister was no longer listening. The sickness was really on him. He never knew how he managed to set the half-finished plate of food on the floor, before he dropped back, with the darkness washing relentlessly over him.

Everything went away, then. He didn't really feel as though he had lost consciousness again, but he knew he must have done so, for when he opened his eyes again a poker game was in progress at the deal table in the crowded center of the room. It seemed to have been going on for some time. After a moment, he tested his strength by propping up on his elbows for a better look.

The players, on crude chairs and boxes, circled the table, with a pack of greasy-looking cards in front of them. They were using bullets from their waist belts for poker chips, but as he lay with the brassy taste of nausea in his mouth and listened to their talk, Jim Bannister began to understand that what they were really playing for were shares in the bounty they planned to collect. Each cartridge, he gathered, stood for a hundred dollars of syndicate money.

Jed Foley appeared to be the heavy winner,

which was hardly surprising; Jed had the brains of the outfit, and as likely as not the greatest skill at cheating. On the far side of the table, young Clay Evans fingered his cards, then shoved a couple more shells into the pot and peered around challengingly. Anger settled coldly through Bannister as he looked at that young and callow face. The kid had a burning cigarette pasted in a corner
of his mouth, but didn't seem quite sure how to handle the smoke that curled up into his face and made one eye blink and water. Bannister saw him cough a time or two, his shoulders heaving.

Morgan Foley won the pot this time, a small one. His brother Jed, gathering in battered cards for the deal, topped the other desultory voices. "One thing I ain't in favor of is letting some stinking peace officer get any part of this. Give them bastards a chance, and there ain't a one but would try to cut himself in for a half, at least!"

There was general agreement. Someone said harshly, "Too bad we can't just cut off his ears and tail and turn them in for the bounty, like a damned lobo wolf! Too bad it ain't that simple!"

Morgan Foley suggested, "Maybe what we should do is send a telegram. Tell the syndicate we got their man, and leave it for them to arrange about picking him up."

"And maybe you think that brass pounder at Cabra Springs would keep his mouth shut?" his brother Hack retorted scornfully. "Hell! The news would be all over these hills in no time. We'd have our hands full, fighting off them that'd like to try and take him away from us!"

Mitch Dekin said, "Then what *are* we going to do?"

"I'll think of something," Jed answered with a shrug; and his brother Morgan added loyally, "Sure, Jed'll think of something."

Clay Evans lifted one shoulder in an eloquent shrug. "All I know," he said, speaking carefully around that cigarette pasted in the corner of his mouth, "is that I sure as hell better get *my* share. Wasn't for me, you wouldn't a one of you so much as—"

The words died on his lips; his head jerked, and then he froze. One by one other heads turned, to look over at the bunk where Jim Bannister was pushing himself to his feet.

"Must have a hard head on him!" Hack Foley started to say, snickering, but he too fell silent at what he saw in Bannister's grim, tight face. Puzzled and unmoving, they watched the prisoner gain his feet, with one big hand clamping the bunk timber to steady himself as the room stopped its pitching. He took a moment to get his weight distributed on his boots; then, deliberately, he started walking toward the table.

Young Evans watched him come, his eyes fixed on Bannister's as though unable to move.

But when the man's arm suddenly lashed forward, hard fist swinging at Evans' startled face, the kid moved fast enough. He let loose a yell and fell away, nearly tumbling off the empty box he was sitting on. He had plenty of time. Bannister's movement was sluggish, lacking steam. Thrown off balance, he staggered against the table and it tilted under his weight, pasteboards slithering and sixgun shells pattering on the floor like rain.

By then the other players were scrambling to their feet, with shouts of anger and alarm. Quickly guns were out of holsters, menacing Bannister; the latter merely looked at them, offering no more fight now. Hack Foley's odd, high-pitched laugh sounded a little nervous.

"Better keep out of his way, kid. Reckon he'd near kill you if he laid hands on you!"

Young Evans gave no answer. He was staring, white faced, at Bannister. Jed Foley said, "Maybe I couldn't blame him, at that. But that's the way it is, Bannister. Your friend, here, sold you out. Ain't a damn thing you can do about it."

The prisoner lifted a hand and ran the fingers through his hair, pushing it back and wincing as he touched that place where the ache in his skull was centered. "I'll tell you what I've decided to do with you," the leader of the Foley clan went on. "We're starting for Denver, come morning. The syndicate's got a branch there. We'll turn you directly over to them and collect our money.

What happens after that is out of our hands. Who knows, you might even get loose again like you did before—but not from us! Give *us* any trouble, and you won't reach Denver alive! Understand?"

When the prisoner made no answer, Hack said gruffly, "I ain't for taking any chances with him at all!"

"Ain't figuring to. Looks like we're gonna have to tie him to make sure he'll be here in the morning. Bring a rope, somebody."

There was one hanging on a nail, a length of new, yellow grass rope, and one of the crew tossed it over. Jed took the rope and tested it by twisting the coils in his hard hands.

Jim Bannister watched, his eyes bleak. He said coldly, "You may as well put a bullet in me now, if you think I'll let you use that on me!"

Hack Foley's eyes turned ugly. "Damn you, you just ain't in any position to say!" His hot words got him no more than a look from the prisoner.

Even though hurt and betrayed and surrounded, like a baited animal at bay, there was something in Jim Bannister that these men couldn't cow. Now he took a breath and, shaking his head as though to clear it, put a slow stare around the bunkroom. "I don't know how you can stand the smell of this place. I don't know how you can stand yourselves!" Abruptly he turned and, shouldering past Mitch Dekin, was moving deliberately, if a little unsteadily, in the direction of the door.

For a moment, caught by pure surprise, no one seemed able to speak. It was Hack who cried hoarsely, "Where the hell do you think you're going?"

"To get me some fresh air," Bannister answered, not looking back. "I've got to clear my head before I start passing out again."

"You come back here!"

But even with their guns trained on his back, Bannister ignored them all. Deliberately he yanked the door open, strode through. And in spite of themselves, they let him go.

CHAPTER XIV

Someone swore: "The nerve of the bastard!" Jarred from his inaction, Jed Foley shook his shoulders and snapped an order at Mitch Dekin, who stood nearest the door. "Damn it, go get him!"

Mitch nodded bruskly and went after Bannister at a run, the shotgun swinging at the end of his gaunt arm.

A lantern had been left burning in the dog-trot passageway that separated the bunkroom from the kitchen, its circle of light swaying as the boisterous night wind rocked it. Mitch hunted quickly and was surprised to discover the big shape of the outlaw leaning motionless against the wall, one hand bracing him; his hanging head and sagging shoulders gave him the look of a man completely spent. Still, an angry suspicion rendered Mitch Dekin alert and dangerous as he came up behind the man with the shotgun ready.

"Don't try any tricks!" He jabbed the bore of the weapon hard against Bannister's meaty back, and the thrust jarred the big man so that his head rolled loosely and wind gusted from his chest. "By God, you best watch your step!" Mitch

Dekin said, louder. "Or you could end up with a tunnel blowed clean through you! Now, turn around!"

Bannister turned, with obvious effort. His face in the swaying lantern light had a look of sickness—shining with sweat, a dribble of dried blood down one cheek from the rip that bludgeoning gun barrel had torn in his scalp. He looked at Mitch Dekin with eyes that scarcely appeared to see him. Suddenly he staggered; the point of a shoulder struck the logs and his knees seemed on the verge of buckling and letting him slide down the wall to the packed dirt of the dog trot.

Faintly alarmed, for all his suspicions, Mitch Dekin took a half step nearer, and in that instant the muzzle of the shotgun moved off its target. It was all the break Bannister needed. With startling suddenness, fingers of steel dropped upon the weapon's polished barrel, trapping it; from the corner of his eye Mitch saw a hand come chopping, hard, toward the side of his neck just below the ear.

He loosed a shout, then tried to pull back and wrench the shotgun free—but succeeded in neither. The edge of the outlaw's palm, hammer hard, struck home; stars exploded across Mitch Dekin's vision and he was going down. Just as the shotgun was wrenched from his hand, his finger cramped the trigger.

Jim Bannister felt the rush of the charge through the metal tube he grasped, as its bellow tore open the night. He cursed the mishap. He had hoped for a weapon, but this one was no good to him without an extra shell for it. He doubted if Mitch would have one on him; and anyway, there was no time to search the man huddled at his feet, because the blast of the explosion had already touched off an uproar on the other side of the log wall.

Bannister couldn't afford to linger, and he didn't. He flung aside the empty weapon, heard it clatter along the packed dirt of the passageway. Then he turned and was running on legs that were far steadier than any of the Foleys might have suspected a minute before. Even so, he had to set his teeth against the blinding stab inside his skull, every time his bootheels struck the ground.

Men were bursting from the house, shouting in excitement and confusion. The lantern swaying on its hook must have hampered their vision; at least there were no gunshots, no rush to overtake him. And Bannister made good use of every second of blundering delay. Ahead, starlight glimmered faintly on the peeled poles of a horse corral; already he was near enough to make out dim shapes stirring uneasily inside. He sprang at the bars, clambered up to straddle the top rail. There he poised, ready to leap as backs and manes and tossing heads moved beneath him.

A light bay hide materialized. It looked like the mount he had seen big Hack Foley riding yesterday—a stocky, deep-barreled animal. Bannister swung out a leg, and dropped. He landed astride, grabbed a handful of mane, as the bay squealed in surprise and moved nervously sideward, in a way that nearly swept Bannister off the broad and unsaddled back and under the ground-trampling hoofs. Sweating, he clamped his knees hard and spoke to try and settle the animal.

Now the other horses had scattered away around the sides of the pen, raising hoofsound and acrid dust. Directly ahead of him he saw what he thought looked like a gate. Bannister reached, located the wire loop that held it closed. He slipped this free and gave the panel a kick that swung it slowly, creaking, wide.

Somebody yelled thinly: *"He's after the horses!"*

With no halter, not even a hackamore, he had almost no control over the bay. But he shouted and used his heels, and the horse joined the frightened mill circling the inner limits of the pen. Moments later the animals had found the open gate, and they went pounding through, crowding Bannister from either side; then they were in the open, running free. Of course, he could not suppose it would take the Foleys long to catch up with them again.

A gun popped somewhere behind him; yells

and the sound of running boots mingled with the clatter of hoofs as the horses scattered. Still another moment and the bay was running alone in the night, with Bannister clinging to its back like a leech.

Suddenly, from nowhere, another fence loomed dead ahead of them. He shouted and tried to pull the bay's head around before they should crash squarely into it. Instead, at the last minute the heavy hind quarters bunched and kicked; the horse took off, floated neatly over the three-railed barrier, and struck the ground beyond with a heavy jarring of bunched hoofs. Bannister was nearly thrown, losing his seat for a heart-stopping moment. It had never occurred to him the horse was a jumper! They were in a stack yard, he guessed. The ghostly shapes of the hay mounds stood about them, and the bay went through them at a run.

Then the farther fence rushed toward them and they were up and over, but this time Bannister was prepared. Even so, it was all he could do to keep his place and his grip in the animal's mane; his head jerked on his neck, snapping his chin hard against his chest when they struck the ground and setting pinwheels spinning inside his skull. He fought against sick dizziness and pain. Now the horse seemed to be running more slowly—climbing, he thought, toward what looked like a black and massive mat of timber.

• • •

He never actually knew at what point he lost the gelding. He supposed a low-hanging branch might have struck him and swept him off its back; or he could simply have lost consciousness. It was night, pitch black under the pines, but he had an idea he must have been lying there for some considerable time. The chill of the earth, still damp from recent rains, had had time to seep deep into him. It was probably the cold that finally roused him, and made him push up to a sitting position, shaking in long, running spasms. The ache in his head was a dull, steady throb.

He thought he must be lying on a narrow trail of some sort, snaking through the scrub-pine growth. There was no sign of the bay, which would have gone on without him or, more likely perhaps, turned back to find its home corral as soon as it realized there was no longer a rider up. In the latter case, the Foleys would probably have picked it up by now and would know he was afoot. They would be searching for him— unless they were waiting for first light, knowing he had small chance of getting away from them in these unfamiliar hills.

He got to his feet and stood with one hand resting against a tree trunk while he tried to sort out his directions. A scatter of stars was visible through the black mass of branches overhead, but not enough to help him judge where he might be with reference to the Foley ranch. As he stood debating, he became aware of sound breaking through the blackness below him—the thud of hoofbeats, coming toward him up the trail.

The steady progress of the single, nearing horse told that it was being ridden. At once Bannister drew back, retreating into the thick timber growth; but unluckily his groping boot came down upon an edge of a rotting log. Bark gave way, tearing loose with a pulpy ripping sound and letting him fall back, crashing, into the branches of a snag before he could catch his balance. He cursed between his teeth.

Below him, the approaching rider had pulled instantly to a halt. He thought he heard saddle leather creak and pop, and the jingle of a bit chain. The forest seemed to breathe in silent waiting.

Then a voice called, cautious and hoarse: "Jim? That you?"

Bannister's mouth drew out long and hard as he recognized the voice, and the muscles of his jaw hardened. He stooped, found a stout length of down timber and straightened silently, hefting it.

The rider drew nearer, a few hesitant paces. "Jim, this is Clay. It's all right, I'm alone. Sing out if you're there."

He could barely see the youngster and the horse, vague dark shapes looming against the blacker background as they came on toward him and halted again. Still he stood motionless, but the horse must have caught the scent, for it snorted suddenly and tossed its head, to the tinkle of a bit chain. Clay Evans interpreted this correctly, for he caught his breath audibly and said again, "You're there, Jim—I know it. But I can't find you if you won't speak out. Please! I want to help you."

At last, Bannister allowed himself to answer. "I guess I'm supposed to believe that!"

The horse pulled quickly to a halt. Leather popped; he could imagine the kid turning in the saddle, searching the darkness for him. "Hell, I know what you're thinkin'," Clay said finally. "And it's a fact—I *did* tell them Foleys about you. But I swear it wasn't for meanin' to. They talked like they meant to kill me—accused me of runnin' with a lawman of some sort, and to save my own hide I had to tell 'em what you really was. And it turned out that smart guy, Jed, knew all about you. He took it from there."

Bannister was unconvinced, and he let it show in unbridled sarcasm. "Sure! I heard the way you were fighting them, to keep from having to take a cut in the reward money!"

"I had to keep 'em fooled, Jim! I had to make 'em think you was nothin' to me but a few bucks on the hoof. That way, maybe there was a chance I could wait for a break and help you get away. Whether you believe it or not, that's the honest to-God truth!"

158

He waited for an answer, and when he got none he said anxiously, "Are you even listening to me?" The horse came on another step or two. One muscled shoulder actually brushed against Bannister, and it occurred to him that he could probably grab Clay Evans, haul the boy from the saddle and disarm him. At the thought, his body tensed.

But then he let the tension run out of him and gave a tired shrug. "All right, kid," he said gruffly. "Maybe I'm a fool, but—I guess I have to believe you." He stepped out into the trail, taking the horse by the bridle to steady it.

Clay Evans let out an exclamation of relief, and quickly swung down. They stood close, barely able to see one another in the thick darkness, and speaking quietly, though there was no one to hear them.

"Where are the Foleys?"

"Scattered out to hunt for you. We caught the bay, so they know you're afoot. How about it, Jim? Are you all right? I thought just maybe you were puttin' all that on, back at the house."

"A half, maybe. I'm still pretty rocky from the clubbing I took."

"You should have a doc look at that." When Bannister only grunted, the kid went on: "Thing we got to do first is get you away from here, before it comes daylight. It'll be too late then.

The Foleys know every foot of these hills; you couldn't hope to lose them!"

"It would be no problem if I only had my sorrel. I left him with the Jackmans, so he's probably at Spur—whatever direction that is." Bannister shook his head in the darkness. "I'm completely lost."

"Well, wait a minute! Seems to me one of the Foleys mentioned Spur was south of here. Looks like that ought to put it somewhere the other side of this ridge. Maybe the trail we're on will take us."

"If it takes us away from the Foleys, that's almost enough."

The kid said, "One way to find out. This old roan of mine carried the pair of us once before, and I reckon he can do it again."

For a moment Bannister hesitated, trying to see Clay Evans' face in the dim, scattered starlight. "I still don't know why you should bother, kid. You don't owe me anything. We haven't exactly been what one would call good friends. I seriously thought you'd be after that reward."

"You helped me out of a tight," the youngster said gruffly. "I ain't so bad off I have to repay a decent turn by playin' Judas. . . . We'll ride better if you take the saddle," he added, abruptly closing the discussion. "I can hang on behind. We'll see if this pile of bones has got anything left in him!"

CHAPTER XV

They saw the ranch buildings from the crest of a rim that put the house and barns and the system of corrals in foreshortened perspective. It was a good location for a cow spread—a tight, protected valley, deeply grassed, walled by timber and watered by a meandering creek. The sun had not yet topped the eastern ridge and the valley lay in shadow, with mists curling from the surface of the creek. The ranch looked to be still asleep as they stood with the horse between them, studying it.

Clay Evans said, "Reckon that's Spur?"

"It would have to be," Bannister said, studying it thoughtfully. "I've heard of no other outfit right in this vicinity."

"There's horses in the pen," the kid said, pointing. "Could be the sorrel's one of them. But in this light I can't make them out."

"No matter. That's Spur, all right."

Jim Bannister turned, preparing to find the stirrup and lift himself again to the saddle, but young Evans' next speech halted him and brought his head up to stare. "Think you can manage alone now? On foot?"

"What do you mean? You're coming with me, aren't you?"

The boy shook his head. "Naw, I don't reckon so. I just wanted to see you made it. Now I have to be heading back, before they start wondering where I've got to."

"You don't mean to tell me you intend going back to the Foleys?"

Doggedly: "It's what I said."

"But—for the love of God, kid! There's no sense in that. You've seen what they are: cheap rustlers and petty thieves! Why would you want to get mixed up again with such a crowd, now that you're free of them?"

Bannister saw the youngster's eyes turn opaque. "Far as that's concerned, I come from the same kind of stock myself. My pa was no better'n them, and I don't reckon there's much likelihood *I'll* ever be. I figure they're about my level."

"Kid, if you really think that, you're a bigger fool than I took you for!"

"Yeah?" Stung, the other's cheeks darkened; he glared at Bannister across the roan's saddle, there in the gray of dawn with the chill breath of morning against them. "Then if I'm a fool, it's my privilege to act like one! All I'm worried about right now is that they shouldn't get suspicious about where the hell I been since midnight. I mean to tell them I got lost in the dark and had to wait till daylight to get my bearings."

"Supposing I won't let you do this?"

"If you don't like the idea, then how about it—would you let me trail with *you?*"

"With me?" Caught short by the question, Bannister could only frown. "You know I can't do that."

Clay Evans nodded, as though this confirmed his argument. "Just how I figured! At least these guys want me. They treat me like I was actually somebody—like I was just as good as them. Nobody else I've met has ever done that. Nobody ever so much as give me the time of day!"

"You're making a mistake," Jim Bannister insisted. But there was really nothing he could do, and he stood helpless as young Evans leaped to the roan's saddle. From there, the boy looked down at him for a moment.

He seemed to be trying to speak; finally he managed: "Good luck!" Then he pulled the horse around and kicked it with his heels. He rode back into the timber, where the dark shadows of the trees quickly swallowed him up. Bannister stood for long minutes, staring after him.

Well, so much for that, he thought regretfully. He wished there were something he could have done for the youngster—some word he might have given. The true irony of it was, he was in no position even to help himself. Clay Evans would have to go his own way, find his own course. After such a start, his future looked bleak enough.

With a shrug for such useless thoughts, Bannister turned and headed down into the valley, following the dim horse track that gave him a semblance of a trail to follow.

It was hard going, through manzanita and scattered pine. The pitch of the hillside was so steep he had to take it slow, since he could not trust his legs that still felt uncertain under him. He stumbled often, over obstacles he should have seen in time to avoid; and more than once he actually fell sprawling and was slow to pull himself to his feet again. Before he had reached the level, the sun had cleared the eastern ridges and was stabbing fingers of light into the valley. It flashed off window glass, made the wet bunch grass shine, turned the mist from the creek to rosy tendrils.

By that time, too, Jim Bannister saw that smoke had begun to rise from the chimney of the silent ranch house; it told him someone was up and kicking life into the banked fire in the stove. But whoever it might be, there was nothing to indicate he had been observed as he came on, doggedly plodding the last distance. He had already determined that one of the horses in the corral was his own sorrel. Now, as he approached the edge of the ranch compound, it moved over and reached its head across the bars to him in greeting. Bannister stopped to speak to it, gave the sleek neck a pat or two while he looked around him.

Spur, on closer view, looked to be a likely enough outfit but rather badly run down. Winter storms had stripped shakes from the house roof and warped the shape of the barn door so that it hung open on its hinges, unable to close. But Bannister saw evidence that someone had been at work here. The barn roof had been mended with gleaming new shakes. A broken rail of the corral had been replaced by one that showed white where the bark was stripped from it. A new beam, jutting from the apex of the barn roof, held the hay pulley and a length of clean yellow rope; the open hay door showed the green of fresh-cut feed stowed there, against the winter that would soon be closing down on this mountain range.

His gear should be in the barn, Bannister thought. He was about to move in that direction when the door of the main house opened and Uncle El Jackman stepped outside—headed for the creek, no doubt, for he had a bucket in his hand. He dropped it with a clatter as he saw the man by the corral. "Bannister!" His cry ran thinly across the morning quiet.

Jim Bannister walked over to him; he could see the reflection of his own appearance in the other's startled look—unshaven, his face and clothing bloody and torn from his flight through the brush.

"Good Lord, man! What's happened to you?"

"It's kind of a long story," Bannister said. "Where are the others?"

"In the house. . . . You've been hurt!" The old man's anxious stare lifted to his face, where dried blood mingled with beard stubble.

Bannister shook his head tiredly. "I'm all right—I think. But I've got to talk to you, all of you. There's things you ought to know. And I may not have much time."

Quickly, leaving the bucket where it had fallen, Uncle El moved to open the door and usher Bannister inside. He ducked the low lintel and stepped across the threshold.

The house seemed to consist chiefly of a single large room that served a double purpose, having a kitchen and eating area fitted out at one end, and a few leather-slung chairs facing a rock-and-mud fireplace at the other to do duty as a living room. The hearth was cold but a fire crackled in the big range. Everything was neat and spotless; the furnishings, he supposed, must have come with the place, except for the few possessions these Jackmans had managed to salvage and bring south with them in their flight from Wyoming. He suspected Tansy Jackman's had been the hand mostly responsible for rescuing the house from neglect and making it once more livable.

A door across the room opened now and Tansy herself entered briskly, just finishing shoving her shirt tail into the waistband of her jeans. She stopped dead at sight of Bannister and pushed the hair back from her eyes.

Uncle El, bustling in behind him, said, "This fellow just blew in. Looks like he's tooken quite a beating."

The girl came slowly forward, halting to look up into Bannister's face with an expression of grave concern and a growing anger. "Was Sid Parrott the one did this?" she cried indignantly. "I'd never have thought—"

"It wasn't Parrott," he told her. "The Foleys. I had another little run in with them."

"The Foleys!"

Boots sounded on the ladder pointing to the loft overhead, where he supposed the men of the Jackman family did their sleeping. Noah Jackman started down. He paused a moment, sharp jealousy leaping into his face as he saw Tansy and Bannister together there below him. His mouth settled and his expression became carefully contained as he climbed down the rest of the way. The three Jackmans stood facing Jim Bannister then, in curiosity that was plainly all but unbearable.

And, standing there, he gave them his news. He passed briefly over the things that had happened to himself, these past thirty hours, came instead directly to the matter which he thought most concerned them—the talk with the lawyer. "I couldn't move him, I'm afraid. He knows nothing of your deal with Sam Murdock, and he cares even less. Murdock told him some story about you folks having agreed to work Spur cattle out of the hills and deliver them to Cabra Springs for a dollar a head. I said it was ridiculous, but he pretended, at least, to believe it. Without proof, I don't think you're going to get anywhere with him."

The Jackmans heard him out with looks of growing discouragement. There was silence for a moment and then Uncle El said heavily, "It's my fault! I always been too trusting, I guess. I let myself believe things would work out, if a man just did his level best. Thinkin' like that, I lost us everything we had in Wyoming. Now it looks like it's gone and happened again."

"No!" Tansy Jackman's lips were set in determination. "It's not fair! Nobody ever worked harder than we have on this job. We got something coming to us, and I won't settle for less. I tell you, I just won't!"

Bannister was touched and, despite his concern, even a little amused by the girl's unquenchable spirit. He had to admire her, but at the same time he couldn't help but wonder what would happen to this girl if she ever once broke—if she were to go down for the count, and lack the resilience to bounce back again.

Noah Jackman asked, "What about this sister

168

of Murdock's—the one that's gonna inherit? You see anything of her?"

"No. Pine told me he was expecting her some time yesterday."

"Think we stand any better chance with her? Or will she just take his advice on everything?"

"If she does, there's not much question what it will be!" Bannister added, "I'm sorry I couldn't bring you better news than this. Afraid I didn't manage to bring back your wagon and team, either."

"Don't worry about that," Tansy assured him; her eyes held a steely glint. "We'll get them ourselves when we go down to town—and I guess that's going to be pretty soon. Things have got to be straightened out with that lawyer man! He hasn't heard the last of us—no matter what he thinks!"

Uncle El fingered his wispy straggle of whiskers, looking vague and indefinite and dispirited. He said, "You *did* tell us that that deputy's gonna be all right?" And at Bannister's nod: "I'm glad to know that, at least. I hate to think of him or anyone else being seriously hurt on account of us. Look at the trouble *you've* had already, just from getting mixed up in our affairs."

"It's not your fault," Bannister protested. "Now, if you've got my outfit that I left with you—"

"Saddle and gear are in the barn," Tansy said.

"You'll find the rest of your belongings in the corner there."

She pointed, and he saw his blanket roll and other meager belongings neatly piled and waiting. Only one important thing gone—his gun and belt, that he'd last seen buckled around Hack Foley's thick middle. This was not the Jackmans' fault, of course, and he didn't mention it, though the knowledge that he must take the trail without any kind of weapon was sobering.

He said only, "There's nothing to hold me, then. The sorrel looks as though it's had a good rest. . . ."

"But *you* don't!" the girl pointed out, frowning anxiously. "You're exhausted, and you've been hurt. Well then, at least," she insisted, when she saw he was about to argue, "let me fix you something to eat. I promise it won't take long— only a minute. Please!"

Bannister hesitated, remembering what her cooking had tasted like and realizing he had had no really solid food since yesterday morning in Sid Parrott's kitchen. He had managed to down precious little of the Foleys' beans and bread. And a man on the run needed a full belly as few others did.

"All right," he said, and nodded. "Thanks. I'm hollow, sure enough." He touched his cheek, stiff with beard stubble and with blood that had dried there. "And it wouldn't hurt me any to clean up a little. I must look like the devil!"

CHAPTER XVI

It was only when he sat at table, with his coat slung across the back of his chair and the rich aroma of the steaming platters in front of him, that Jim Bannister realized how nearly starved he really was. The nausea from that blow on the skull was completely gone now, leaving him nothing worse than a dull ache and a deep lethargy that settled more firmly upon him once he let himself relax to the comfort and warmth of the friendly room.

Though he knew he should be riding, he found himself lingering where he was even after Noah and Uncle El had tramped out of the house on some chore of their own—the younger man going with a dark backward look. Tansy Jackman got up to refill Bannister's coffee cup for him, then replaced the battered pot on the stove and sat down in her chair again. She folded her arms and leaned both elbows on the table, in such a way that—no doubt unconsciously—her full, firm breasts swelled the front of the man's shirt she wore. She frowned, looking full into his face, and blurted a thought that must have been much on her mind.

"Twelve thousand dollars is an awful lot of

reward money! Did you really kill a syndicate man?"

Bannister spooned sugar from a glass jar into his cup. "I killed three." He saw her eyes darken with beginning horror. "Two were hired gun-slingers," he said in explanation. "I never troubled my conscience about that pair, in particular."

"But—the third one?" She added quickly, "You don't have to tell me. It's none of my business. . . ."

He shrugged, picked up the cup, and set it down again, frowning at dark memories. "I guess I'd rather you knew about me, than imagine things that might be worse than the truth."

So, briefly, he told her of the trouble a year ago, down in New Mexico Territory. He told her about the man named McGraw, field agent for the Western Development Corporation of Chicago, who had decided his company needed Jim Bannister's one-man horse ranch to piece out a land title. Bannister and his wife had talked it over and decided they were not going to sell, merely to satisfy some big-money combination; but the syndicate man was not used to being thwarted. He sent two thugs with guns to convince them.

Bannister told of that terrible night when his stock was slaughtered, and the torch put to his house and buildings and haystacks—and when a careless bullet from one of the syndicate guns had hit his wife and left her dying in his arms. Tansy listened, horrified, and, as she saw the agony that pinched his lips, giving his craggy face a look of pure tragedy, she said in a small voice, "Those were the men you killed?"

He nodded, his eyes bleak. "I killed them— the same way I'd step on a scorpion. And then I went after McGraw, the man who'd sent them. I trailed him to a hotel in Las Vegas. I won't go into details of what happened, except that he pulled a gun—and when it ended, he was dead. I stood trial for murder."

"But surely, after what had gone before—"

"The syndicate ran that trial to please themselves. They were determined to make an example of me, just to show what could happen to anyone who dared stand up against them. They sent a battery of their top lawyers to help with the prosecution; they probably even reached some of the jury." He shrugged. "Anyway, they got the conviction they wanted. Only I didn't wait to be hanged. A guard got careless, and I broke jail. I've been on the dodge ever since."

She was watching his face, her lips parted, pure sympathy coloring her eyes. "Jim! How terrible! How long can you go on like this?"

"Well, it gets a little harder all the time, as the word about me spreads. At the price the syndicate's put on me, there's plenty that will go out of the way to help them." He took a final drag at the coffee cup, set it down. But then one of his rare smiles broke across his face. "I'm not asking you to worry about me. Things aren't completely hopeless. Given a break, I figure I might even get that conviction set aside."

"But how? With everyone dead against you?"

"Not quite everyone, maybe. Even on the dodge, a man picks up a friend or two."

"You've got *us!*" she exclaimed, and impulsively she reached out and seized his hand with her own, where they lay on the table between them—his big, hard hand clutched in her small brown paw. Suddenly she became aware of what she was doing, for she colored slightly and hastily snatched her fingers back again. "But a lot of good we could ever do you," she said. "We don't even seem able to help ourselves."

Jim Bannister told her, "You're a good friend, Tansy. I'll never forget that."

Her color deepened; pleased and embarrassed, she all of a sudden appeared not to know where to look. An alarming thought crossed Bannister's mind: I believe this girl thinks she's in love with me!

To get past a ticklish moment, he returned to the matter under discussion. "The syndicate people deny that any agent of theirs would be guilty of the things I accused McGraw of doing. But I think it's possible they can be proved wrong. Three months ago, over at a town called

Antelope, I managed to corral one of the top men in the organization, a fellow named Selden, and made him listen to my side of the story. I argued that the company might have been deceived in the kind of agents they had working for them. I suggested there were ways he might check up on McGraw and his gunmen, maybe learn about other such jobs they'd pulled, for other outfits.

"I don't know for sure if I impressed him, but at least Selden halfway promised he'd see if he could find any grounds for reopening my case. Maybe nothing will come of it; still, I've got to give him time—and meanwhile manage to stay out of the hands of the bounty hunters."

"Where will you go when you leave here?"

"It's probably better if you don't know. Besides, I don't really know myself. There were a couple of men on my trail when I came into this country; I hope I've lost them. I'm going to have to try and make sure." He got to his feet as he spoke. He was immediately astounded by the reaction of his body—every muscle seemed to protest, and his knees were so lacking in stiffness that he found himself clutching the back of his chair for support. At once the girl was up, facing him in alarm. "You shouldn't be riding!" she exclaimed. "That blow you took is still troubling you."

"Nonsense," he muttered. "That was hours ago." But he touched the hurt, under the square of court plaster Tansy had put on it. "I can't let a thing like this lay me out. Once I get started I'll be all right."

The sun was high, by now, and flooding the room. It was alarming to see how time had been moving away from him as he lingered here. Yet, despite the urgency he felt to be on his way, something warned him that the girl was right and he was foolish to press himself too hard. He made no protest when she laid a hand on his sleeve and told him, "You're going to rest now. No one knows you're here—not the Foleys, or the sheriff, or anyone else. We'll keep a watch; I promise you'll be safe. Please! Let us do this much for you."

He looked down at her for a long moment, and slowly moved his head in agreement. "All right. An hour, perhaps. Not a minute longer."

"We'll see. . . ."

He let himself be led to the door of that room where, earlier, he had seen her emerge. It was barely large enough to hold an old brass bed and a chest of drawers. A curtain hung in a corner, forming a closet of sorts. "My room," she said. "You'll be all right here."

He got to the bed, let himself down on the edge of it. When he started to pull off a boot she made a move as though she would do it for him; outraged, he shook his head and waved her away. With a smile she turned to the door. Her hand on the knob, she said, "Sleep if you can—please don't be afraid to. I'm sure it's what you need."

"I'm sure you're right."

Still she lingered, looking at him. There was something more she wanted to say; she finally got it out: "What was her name, Jim? Your wife?"

"Her name?" A fleeting, remembered pain pulled at the corner of his mouth and touched his eyes. "Marjorie."

"You loved her very much?"

Bannister nodded, not looking at her. "Yes. Very much."

"I was sure of it." Tansy Jackman started to say something more. Then, instead, she quietly drew the door to and left him there alone.

The woman who had introduced herself as Sam Murdock's sister was completely baffling to Claude Pine. She was a tiny creature, frail and faded, and resembling her dead brother too closely ever to have looked like much. She looked, in fact, like a natural-born old maid. Yet she had been married, some thirty years ago, to an army sergeant who had promptly got himself killed in the line of duty. Pine gathered, from such little as Kate Harper told him, that Sam had disapproved of the match; brother and sister had never so much as met in the time since she became a widow.

She lived on a tiny pension and on what she made by managing a rooming house—though where she found the strength for such hard work, one could wonder, looking at the woman's thin frame and the patient, rather horsey features. He would have expected to find her tired out from her journey. Far from it! The first thing she said was that she wanted to finish her business here as quickly as possible. She was too busy a woman to spend time gadding. The house wouldn't run itself while she was gone.

She went to the lawyer's office and spent an hour looking through the musty ledger books and other papers he got out for her, putting on a pair of hornrimmed spectacles to do so. She listened to all he had to say, with no comment except to ask an occasional question that showed nothing was escaping her. That done, she announced she would like to look over the property she was inheriting in Downey. Pine hired a rig from the livery, and took her around to inspect the three business buildings and the mill, and the grubby little row of millhands' houses from which she would be drawing rent. He had the impression that her mild and slightly myopic eyes missed no detail.

"Thank you so much, Mr. Pine," she said afterward. "Now, if I may, I'd like to take a look at the store."

He blinked. "The store? But Mrs. Harper! That's

ten miles out of town! Shouldn't it wait till morning?"

The woman fixed him with a look of unmistakable meaning. "Mr. Pine," she said primly. "I don't know about *you,* but I have told you before, I am a busy woman! This is no pleasure trip for me. I realize I am being a nuisance, but I simply cannot see wasting nearly half a day. Not with one of those lazy tenants of mine likely to burn the house down in my absence."

The lawyer sighed. He refrained from commenting that a woman as wealthy as she stood to be, once Sam Murdock's estate was finally settled, could just as well afford to set fire to that rooming house herself. He went looking for Harry Jones, located him in a saloon where Jones and some of the other thwarted manhunters were heatedly discussing their failure to bag Jim Bannister. Pine hauled the man out of there, put him on his horse and sent him ahead to open up the store. He and Kate Harper followed in the buggy, getting there as a mountain sunset was shaping up.

Claude Pine was somehow not surprised when, having made a survey of buildings and equipment, the woman announced that she wanted to take inventory on the spot. They got to the job after a hasty supper—Harry Jones and the lawyer clambering around over shelves and bins, raising a choking dust, while Mrs. Harper primly made lists in an old-maidish, copper-plate hand. When the long job was completed, toward midnight, she showed her weariness in heightened pallor and a deepening of the lines about her eyes and mouth.

But as she thanked both men for their help, folding the sheets of paper to place in her reticule, she added, "Now, Mr. Pine. You mentioned something about a cattle ranch. I suppose we can see this tomorrow?"

The attorney suppressed a martyr's groan. "It's a long ride, ma'am. Into the mountains."

Nearsighted eyes met his, blandly, behind the thick lenses of her spectacles. "Then I suppose we had better get as early a start as possible, hadn't we?"

An early start, to Kate Harper, meant predawn blackness. Starting up the pass road, enduring the mountain chill and fighting a restless buggy team, Claude Pine eyed a pileup of clouds around the higher peaks and hoped they wouldn't be running into more weather. He saw no use in mentioning the possibility to the woman beside him, knowing by now it would have no effect at all. Nor did he see any point in reminding her again of what he had told her about the Foleys, though he was glad that his snubnosed revolver, fully loaded, was in a pocket of his coat, underneath the heavy mackinaw he had donned against the cold morning.

Apparently he needn't have worried. The skies cleared, the rented buggy held together, the horses made good time. It was still something short of noon when their road brought them, by an easy grade, into the end of the valley where Spur head-quarters stood. They followed the twisting course of the creek, over flats where grass stood rank and yellow, now, after the first frosts. Aspen ran tongues of yellow up the creases in the shouldering ridges; the noon air was crystal clear.

The woman said, "Shouldn't there be some cattle?"

"I've already explained that. The stock's scattered in the hills, a lot of it unbranded. Sam took book count, without asking for an actual tally. The owner was anxious enough to sell to make the price a bargain in any case."

"He was frightened out, you say?"

"By the Foleys. That's right."

"And now there's these other people, this Jackson family—"

"Jackman."

She acknowledged the correction. "They appear to think they can move in on a defenseless widow woman and take over for themselves. I believe you told me they even dared give protection to the outlaw who murdered my brother. They must be a choice lot!"

"As for that," Claude Pine said, pointing with

the buggy whip, "you can decide for yourself. There they are now."

The buggy had rolled in off the grass, into the hard-packed, week-grown ranchyard. Pine could see the woman looking around her curiously, taking it all in. And yonder the little group of people by the hay barn stood waiting, motionless, as the newcomers approached.

There were three of them—the old man with whiskers, and the two younger ones. He heard the woman say suddenly, "Why, one of them's a girl!"

It was understandable she should be surprised—or appalled—at the effrontery of a female who had such a lack of shame as to dress like that. Pine drew rein and made the introductions. "These are the Jackmans. . . . Mrs. Harper is the new owner of this property."

The wispy-looking old man with the beard bobbed his head. "Morning, ma'am. Sort of figured it would be you."

Apparently the three of them had been rehanging the door. A new crossbrace had been nailed on, to pull it into shape, and now the girl and her uncle were helping to hold it steady while the younger man reset the hinge nails. The latter stood with the screwdriver still poised in his hand.

"I'm Tansy Jackman," the girl said, and stepped forward with a hand extended tentatively. But the woman on the buggy seat was looking elsewhere and failed to see it, and Tansy let it drop again.

Kate Harper gave the ranchyard and the buildings a slow and thorough surveyal. She brought her prim glance back to the three as she said, in a dry tone, "You people certainly seem to have been making yourselves at home."

"We had every right," Tansy Jackman said defensively. "Our deal with Mr. Murdock—"

"Was no deal at all, as far as I'm concerned!" Claude Pine cut her off. "I should warn you that I've advised Mrs. Harper to pay no heed to any demands you people might make of her."

"I understand," the woman said, before Tansy Jackman could make an angry retort, "that you claim my brother offered you an interest in this ranch—for nothing!"

The girl corrected her indignantly. "It wasn't for nothing, Mrs. Harper. It was for taking over and making Spur a paying spread. And for holding off those maneating Foleys while we did it!"

Noah Jackman spoke up. "That's the Lord's truth, ma'am! We've about broke our hearts on this job. It ain't fair we should be booted out now—just when we were beginning to get somewhere." His stepfather nodded solemn agreement.

Tansy added defiantly, "You just ought to of

seen this place before we moved in! We deserve something, if only fair wages for the time we've already put in."

The two people in the buggy exchanged a look, and the lawyer lifted one shoulder slightly—as though the Jackman family's claim could be dismissed with a gesture. "We'll discuss all this later. Just now, Mrs. Harper wants to have a look at the rest of her property." He touched up his team with the leathers.

As the buggy rolled on toward the house, Tansy Jackman suddenly gasped and began an impulsive move forward, but it went unnoted. Claude Pine drove straight over the yard, bringing his rig to a halt beneath the single tall, old cottonwood whose branches, with a few yellow leaves still clinging, laid their shadows across the roof of the main building. He got down, took a weight strap from the buggy and snapped it to the bridle of the near horse. Afterward he helped Kate Harper to alight, and guided her up the broad steps to the gallery.

By now all three of the Jackmans had left the barn and were coming across the weed-grown yard; Tansy herself suddenly broke into a run.

Pine and the woman stepped across the threshold. After the crisp autumn chill, this room was warm and cheerful from the fire that crackled in the big range. A fine aroma drifted from a soup kettle simmering on the back of the stove. Kate

Harper sniffed and lifted her brows, with a glance at the lawyer.

"She's a good cook, at least."

He merely shrugged, and walked into the room. "Loft," he said, pointing to the ladder leading to a square hole in the ceiling. He saw a second, closed door and started for it. "This should be a bedroom. . . ."

Even as his hand fell upon the china knob, he almost imagined he heard a faint movement, a squeal of bedsprings. He twisted the knob, gave it a shove that sent the door wide. And then he halted, to stare at the man who stood with one hand resting on a knob of the heavy brass bedstead.

For a moment, neither moved. Suddenly the lawyer's smoothly fleshy face turned red with fury. He grabbed for the pocket of his suitcoat, fumbling during an alarming instant as the mackinaw got in his way; then the hand dived inside, and there was an exclamation from Kate Harper when it came out gripping a snubnosed revolver.

"All right!" Pine heard his own voice saying, hoarsely. "Don't try anything, Bannister—anything at all. Because if you do, you're dead."

Only then did it occur to him he faced an unarmed man.

CHAPTER XVII

Jim Bannister's first thought was that he must look very much a fool, standing there helplessly clutching the bedstead, blinking at the gun pointed in his face. Normally he would neve have been caught like this. It was the final, lingering effect of the clubbing he had taken, making him slow to wake when the sentinel in his ear caught the sound of the outer door opening, and of voices that didn't belong here.

With all the best intentions, Tansy Jackman must have let him sleep far beyond the single hour she'd promised. It was probably just what he needed; already the fog was dissipating, and he was conscious of a new strength and alertness. The worst was over. But nothing could cause this redfaced and furious man in the doorway, or the gun in his fleshy hand, to vanish. Claude Pine's lips were drawn tight as he gestured with the gun and said sharply, "Move on out of there!"

"You'll have to wait till I get my boots," Jim Bannister said.

Ignoring the weapon, he seated himself on the edge of the bed while he proceeded to pull them on. Actually he was casting about, hunting for a possible break; but nothing suggested itself.

Finally, impatient and suspicious, the lawyer challenged him: "You're stalling! Now get on your feet."

Bannister sighed and stood up. The other's plainly high-strung manner prompted him to remark, "Just be careful with that thing!"

"*You* be careful," the lawyer retorted, "about keeping both your hands where I can see them."

There was no use resisting a drawn gun. Bannister moved through the door and into the main room, with his captor backing cautiously to make way for him. And now the woman who stood to one side, discreetly watching all this, asked a question of the lawyer. "Did you say his name is Bannister?"

He had scarcely noticed her. Now he looked at her curiously, wondering who this drab little person might be, with her worn hands and her plain features that rather resembled those of a sheep. He was quickly enlightened.

"But Mr. Pine!" she exclaimed. "Wasn't that the name—"

"Of the one that murdered your brother," the lawyer finished for her, nodding. "In addition to a few other people. Quite right."

Bannister thought: But naturally—the sister; Sam Murdock's heir. She couldn't have been anyone else.

Claude Pine turned on him again, his eyes hotly

vindictive. "You must have thought I wouldn't know you, yesterday! You must have considered yourself very clever, to walk into my office the way you did, and make a fool of me!"

So something else was cleared up. It was injured pride, and not so crass a thing as the reward, that was motivating this man. Very possibly, thought of the money hadn't yet entered his head. Jim Bannister returned his bitter stare but made no answer.

The man was angry enough already. Anything Jim said would probably do nothing but further antagonize him.

Footsteps were pounding on the gallery now; the door burst wide and Tansy Jackman stood framed there, breathless, with her cousin Noah and the old man crowding close behind. Claude Pine, not looking around or letting his gun waver from the prisoner, spoke impatiently across a shoulder. "Well, come in! Come in! But I'm warning you: Don't try to interfere!"

Jim Bannister saw the instant understanding and dismay that showed on the girl's face and drained it of color. Slowly the Jackmans came on into the room, and Uncle El closed the door.

"I'm afraid the sheriff's due for a disappointment," Claude Pine was saying, a trifle smugly. "He swears up and down you people couldn't have known what Jim Bannister was, the other day when you lied to cover up for him. But even if you didn't know then, you've learned since. No use denying it!"

Bannister ground his teeth. "Let them alone!" he snapped, suddenly unable to hold it back. "Don't try to make criminals of them on account of me! They're simply decent people, who don't enjoy seeing someone else in a tight place. Besides, they thought they owed me a favor."

"No one is bound to do favors," the other insisted, doggedly, "for a man that's put himself outside the law!" He looked at Kate Harper. "I hope now you're ready to take my advice. If you don't want your ranch turned into a refuge for criminals, you'll get these people out of here directly."

The woman nodded. "Yes," she said, clipping her words. "I'm afraid I have to agree."

Jim Bannister saw that hit the Jackmans; for once Tansy Jackman looked stunned beyond arguing, but poor Uncle El took the news in such shock that his whole face seemed to crumple. He shook his head, crying out his protest.

"No! You can't just kick us out like this! We got no other place to go. . . ." His mouth began to work; suddenly tears were spilling over the rims of his eyes and down his cheeks.

Noah, turning to him, took the old man by an elbow and shook it gently. "Don't beg, Pa," he said. "Let's keep our dignity. Don't worry; I

189

can find work. I'll take care of you and Tansy."

The old fellow accepted the reprimand. He nodded, shamefaced.

And Tansy, with lips set and white, turned to Kate Harper. "Don't worry! We'll be leaving just as soon as we can manage. You'll have to give us time, though, to fetch our wagon from town and load our belongings."

The woman nodded. "Of course."

"And what happens to Jim Bannister?"

"That's none of your concern," Claude Pine told her crisply. He looked at his prisoner who, with arms still raised, was beginning to get an ache across the shoulders. "Has this man got a horse?"

After a pause, Noah Jackman reluctantly answered. "Yeah. In the corral."

"One of you put a saddle on it and bring it over. Meanwhile, I smell something good there on the stove. Mrs. Harper and I haven't eaten since before daylight; so, I think we'll invite ourselves to join you. After all, it's her kitchen."

Kate Harper frowned a little. "I really don't think there was any call to put it that way."

"Certainly not," Tansy said, barely able to keep her voice civil. "You're welcome to what we have. . . ."

She gave the lawyer a chilly stare and turned away, to begin setting out dishes from the packing case that did service as a cupboard. Claude Pine told his prisoner suspiciously, "All right, I guess you can lower your hands now—but don't think I'll be taking my eyes off you. I'm not doing that until I see you turned over to the sheriff. That is a promise!"

The old roan horse seemed to be growing resigned to the strange way its rider was acting. Bony flanks were lathered from fighting the up-and-down slants, sometimes without even a hint of a trail, and continuously hampered by these drunken swayings in the saddle. Twice within the hour the roan had wandered into rocky cul-de-sacs and stood waiting patiently to be shown the way out again. Now, having picked its way uneasily down a slope, it had finally stopped to graze.

The rider seemed to be paying no heed at all, any more; every time the roan dipped its head, the weight on its back shifted perilously forward. The old horse drifted about, tearing at the rank grass. A cluster of ranch buildings in the middle distance seemed to lie dozing in autumn sun-light.

But at last the rider straightened, saddle leather creaking under him; he hauled in the reins, pulling his animal's head up despite tough-jawed resistance. "Come on, horse!" he mumbled. "I'm havin' enough trouble; please don't give me any more! We're almost there." After a snort of protest, the old horse went ambling ahead.

They entered the ranchyard and lagged to a halt under the big cottonwood in front of the house. The rider lifted his voice: "Jim? Hello!" His only answer was the wind that rustled the few remaining leaves on the branches overhead. He tried again, with greater effort: "Jim Bannister! Please—*somebody*. . . ."

The door was flung open and Bannister came striding, fast, out to the horse and the rider clinging on its back. He barely made it; Clay Evans was already beginning to lose the saddle. He sagged weakly sideward, fell directly into Bannister's arms, and lifted a face that had been battered nearly shapeless, and as bloody as a steak.

"Jim?" he said hoarsely.

Without a word, Bannister got the weight of him into his arms. He brushed past Claude Pine and the Jackmans, got the boy inside the house and to a chair at the table, where he gently lowered his burden, while someone else cleared aside the remains of the interrupted meal.

"Kid! Can you hear me?"

Clay Evans was trying to peer at him from eyes that were all but invisible behind cut and swollen lids. Sickened, Bannister thought: Whoever did this must have concentrated on his face! He looked around at the others and demanded irritably, "Can't you give us a little air?"

Tansy had hurried away and was back now,

carrying a tin basin filled with warm water from the stove, and a clean cloth over her arm. But the boy pushed her away. "No!" Clay lurched convulsively in the chair. "There's no time!"

Bannister laid a hand on his shoulder. "Yes there is. Tell us who cut you up like this. Looks to me like Hack Foley's work."

The boy's head wobbled as he tried to nod. "You were right all along, Jim—and I was a damn fool! I thought the Foleys liked me. They wasn't interested in nothing but the bounty they thought I could help 'em get for you." He rocked his head in self-accusation and despair. "Why the hell didn't I listen when—"

"Slow down, now. Start at the beginning. What happened?"

Clay Evans took a shuddering breath. "When I got back to the Foleys this morning, I tried hard to stall for you. I told 'em I'd seen you heading west, but after they'd wasted a couple of hours hunting for sign, Hack finally smelled a rat. He figured I was lying, and he set out to beat the truth out of me. Even after I broke down and talked, the bastard kept right on hittin'. . . ."

Bannister's eyes were hard, his lips set in a tight line. "It sounds like him. They know I came here, then?"

"I'm sorry, Jim. I—I had to tell, or they'd of killed me! Besides, I figured you ought to be long gone before this."

193

"It's all right, boy. That wasn't what I meant. You got nothing to apologize for."

"But you haven't heard it all!" The boy pulled himself up a little, in his urgency pawing at Bannister's sleeve. "Just to make sure, they sent Mitch Dekin over for a look and he reported seeing that sorrel of yours, still here in the corral. So now they're comin' after you!"

"And you rode all this distance to warn me? Beat up the way you are?" Jim Bannister straightened, to look soberly down at the youngster. "Kid, I appreciate this—more than you can know!"

"Forget it," Clay Evans said gruffly. "The thing is, I lost so much time it's a pure wonder they didn't arrive first. You and me, we better skin out of here!"

Bannister turned his head, seeking out Claude Pine's uncompromising stare; he saw the lawyer's hand thrust deep in that bulging pocket, and his own mouth quirked in a bleak suggestion of a smile. "Afraid that would be a little hard to manage, right at the moment. . . ."

"You think this is some kind of a joke?" the boy demanded fiercely; he had seen the smile and misunderstood it. "Lemme tell you! They've went and called up the whole outfit—should be eight or nine altogether, I figure. The rest was passing the jug while they waited around for them, and they kind of forgot about me; that's how come I was able to sneak out."

"Eight or nine?" Claude Pine sounded as though the idea amused him. "Just to take one man? Bannister ought to feel flattered."

"Oh, they want Bannister, all right. But that ain't the only thing."

"What else, then?"

"Why, it's this here ranch—Spur. It's a real thorn in their hide. From what I heard, them Foleys are apt to be running two, maybe three holdings of stolen beef at the same time. They can't risk neighbors so close, working the same range, probably finding out what they're doing.

"You'll remember," the boy went on, "the guy that first started this spread got run out. They tried the same treatment on the Jackmans, but it didn't work so good. Now, though, they say Spur's gone and played right into their hands by taking in Jim Bannister. Since he's wanted by the law, Jed Foley's decided this is all the excuse they need to bring their whole crew over here. They'll get Bannister, and burn the place while they're at it."

Noah Jackman got to his feet, staring. *Burn* it?"

"To the ground! They intend to bag Jim Bannister and be quit of you people, all at once—and claim, if anybody asks 'em, they were just doin' the law's work."

There was a moment's shocked reaction, a prolonged and silent trading of looks. Uncle El spoke huskily. "Do they really imagine Sid Parrott would hold still for that?"

"It'll all be over and done before the sheriff even knows. Jed figures he won't be able to do anything about it then." Clay Evans shrugged. "Look, I'm only sayin' what I heard—whether you happen to believe me or not."

For some reason they all looked at Bannister then. "Tell us, Jim," Tansy Jackman urged. "What do *you* think?"

He frowned; he said slowly, "I think I believe him. The whole thing sounds crazy enough, but it's just the sort of notion Jed Foley might come up with."

Suddenly Noah Jackman was whirling and heading for the door; he jerked it open and strode outside, to put an anxious stare at the rim where an attacker should first be expected to appear. He pivoted slowly, looking all around the encircling ridges. As he came back in, Tansy met him with a question: "Any sign of them?"

"Not yet."

Claude Pine said, in a contemptuous tone, "I still don't see what you're getting excited about. Those Foleys aren't as dangerous as all this. Hardly more than a bunch of illiterate savages— generally drunk, any time I see them, on cheap popskull whiskey!"

Noah Jackman didn't bother to answer. His face grim, he moved directly to a glass-fronted case and opened the doors, revealing within the gleam of a couple of rifles. He lifted one of these out, found a box of shells and began feeding them into the weapon's breech. The lawyer said, "I wonder what he thinks he's doing now?"

"What does it look like he's doing?" Jim Bannister retorted. "He's getting ready to make a stand!"

Uncle El, too, after the briefest indecision, had joined his stepson and with trembling hands was lifting the other rifle out of the case. This was an old Spencer repeater that looked almost too heavy for him to manage.

Pine said, "But why should it matter to them? They've been ordered off the place."

Bannister looked at him. "Didn't you even see the job they've done here? The new shakes for the roof, that barn door, all the rest of it? Even you should understand that, after so much work, it wouldn't be easy to walk away and let somebody put a torch to it."

Tansy Jackman had vanished briefly into the bedroom. Now she was back, and she too had a weapon—a small pearl-handled revolver. But Bannister intercepted her and gently but firmly lifted it from her fingers. "Oh, no!" he said, when she protested. "If there's any shooting done, you're not going to be in it!"

Claude Pine, whose reactions appeared a trifle slow, suddenly seemed aware that the prisoner had a gun in his hand. His own revolver gave a convulsive leap and he exclaimed harshly, "Here! Here, now!" But as Bannister started to turn, a movement at the other end of the room caught the lawyer's eye. His head came around, and there was Noah Jackman's rifle, pointed casually in his direction.

The sandyhaired man said, with no particular emphasis, "Something bothering you, lawyer?"

Pine looked at him, and at the rifle, and a muscle began to twitch under the smooth skin on his jaw; Bannister thought he might be about to have a stroke. But then, slowly, while the rest of the people in the room watched in silence, he let the hand with the gun in it lower to his side.

Jackman said, "You know, your buggy and team's still out there. Maybe you ought to just take 'em and git."

"No!" The attorney's face had gone red and he was having some trouble with his breathing, but he spoke firmly enough. "You're not getting rid of me! I'm not afraid of you—or of the Foleys, either. Still, I guess my business with Jim Bannister can wait until after this other thing has been taken care of." And he dropped the revolver back into his pocket.

Noah Jackman only grunted, and turned to Bannister, who was studying him in some amazement. Twice now, he was thinking, this fellow had swallowed his personal dislike long enough to attempt doing him a favor: the first time by offering to drive that wagon with the hurt deputy in it down to the county seat. Now he ignored Bannister's nod of thanks and said, "Shall I put the horses in the barn, then?"

"Corral might be better," Bannister suggested. "If the Foleys should hit the barn, I'd rather see the horses run off than have them caught in a fire trap."

"That makes sense," Noah said, and went out. His stepfather, calling, "I'll lend you a hand with them," followed quickly after, lugging the heavy Spencer under one frail arm.

Bannister looked to the weapon he had taken from the girl. It was a .32, light of frame and nearly engulfed in his big hand. He rocked the cylinder out, saw it was fully loaded, clicked it shut again. Tansy was at the window, anxiously peering up at the timbered ridge. And now Clay Evans said, through puffed and bleeding lips, "Anybody have an extra gun? I'm gonna settle with that Hack Foley if it's the last thing I do!"

He started to get his feet under him, but Kate Harper laid a hand on his shoulder and told him firmly, "What you're going to do right now, young man, is sit where you are while I try to fix up that poor face of yours."

"But—"

"I said be quiet!" Her voice held surprising

authority. The boy settled back, scowling, and she picked up the cloth Tansy had left lying on the table, ripped off a length with a sound like a pistol shot and dipped it into the pan of warm water. As she began gently dabbing at the bloody welts, she spoke over her shoulder. "Find something I can put on these cuts."

"Yes, ma'am," Tansy Jackman said meekly, and went looking for it in the cupboard. Bannister, watching the woman working over Clay Evans, saw the way her homely face twisted in sympathy when he winced at her touch. The water in the pan quickly began to take on a reddish tinge. She could have been a mother tending to her own son—or, it occurred to him, perhaps more accurately—an affection-starved and childless woman giving expression to some deep inner need.

Once she said, as the boy's whole face contracted in a grimace, "I hope I'm not hurting you too much."

"No ma'am. It feels good." He looked up when she paused to tear another length of cloth. He said suddenly, "I guess you must be old man Murdock's sister?" She nodded. But when she would resume her work, he lifted a hand to stop her. "Wait! There's something I better tell you."

Alarm prompted Jim Bannister to exclaim: "No, kid, don't! Let it go."

But, doggedly, the boy persisted. "I'm the one that killed Sam." The woman stiffened; her eyes flew wide. "Yes, ma'am. Sheriff thinks Bannister done it, but—I'm afraid it was me. I never meant to; that's the truth. It—just happened."

Bannister watched the struggle of emotion on the woman's face, looking at young Evans in pure shock and disbelief and then something like horror. She started to draw back, as though she would not let herself touch him. But with the next breath her expression altered subtly. She seemed to retreat behind the lids of her nearsighted eyes as she spoke, in a nearly tone-less voice.

"We'll discuss it later—but thank you, at least, for telling me. Now, hold still. . . ."

And then Noah Jackman was back, with Uncle El trembling at his heels. "It's them!" the young fellow shouted. "It's the Foleys! They're comin', all right—and it looks like they got an army with them."

CHAPTER XVIII

Standing full in the sun, only a pattern of bare cottonwood branches between, Bannister thought with strange irrelevance, I must have lost my hat somewhere. He raised an arm to shield his eyes and now he could see a knot of horsemen out there on the yellow expanse of grass. They had halted for some reason that was, at the moment, a mystery to him. But now they came on, and the confused clot of shapes broke apart and he was able to count them—seven riders. No, eight. Sunlight winked from gun barrels, from the metalwork of saddles and bit chains. The group lifted to a gallop, yet it was as though they drew no closer, but merely swelled in size, the legs of the horses scissoring as though in slow motion against the yellow grass, the drum of hoofs growing louder, interspersed by a high, drunken whooping.

He saw then that three or four men carried something besides guns. Smoke made a smudge of oily black from rags burning at the ends of wooden stakes. That was the reason they had halted—to soak their firebrands and set them alight. Once or twice, now, Bannister thought he heard the rhythmic banging of a kerosene tin, tied to a saddle.

Behind him, in the doorway, he heard Noah Jackman's voice, husky with emotion: "The kid was right! They really mean to do it! They mean to burn us out!"

Over his shoulder Bannister had a glimpse of Claude Pine watching at a window. From the look of the man's face, he seemed to have lost all his arrogant disdain of the Foleys; he looked very scared. Jim Bannister, for his part, could feel the breath thicken in his throat, for all at once he was remembering another time and another place when he had watched other riders who came like these, brandishing torches. But if cold sweat broke suddenly on his forehead and his palms, it was anger and not fear that set him trembling.

He called back to those in the house: "We're going to have to shoot our way out of this one! Don't take any chances. Drunk or not, a man with a gun or a torch in his hand is nobody to fool with!"

He looked around the yard, checking the stock pen, with the horses inside and the lawyer's rented buggy parked nearby. There was not much they could do about it if the Foleys took it into their heads to run off the horses. Then his eye passed on to the big hay barn opposite, and a shocking thought struck him. That barn, with the cutting of winter feed stored in the mow, offered a prime target—and it was completely undefended.

Without stopping to consider the wisdom of it, Bannister was already heading at a run across the compound. The earth seemed almost to shake under him, now, to the beat of the nearing horses, but they were still far enough that he made the barn with time to spare. He plunged inside, then glanced around, hunting for someplace where he could fort up. Then he saw the ladder climbing to the haymow and he leaped at it, went scrambling upward. The big hay door stood half closed. He pushed it wide, and discovered he had a clear vantage point overlooking the entire ranchyard.

In the next instant, the raiders hit Spur and pulled in from their headlong rush.

Bannister thought: If they aren't too drunk they'll be looking for a trap; they'll be wondering where the hell everybody is. In any event they didn't spend long at it. For there was Jed Foley, standing in the stirrups, holding a rifle by its balance as he bawled orders. At once a couple of the riders peeled off and were spurring straight for the main house, whooping like boys in a game and swinging their torches for the cast that would send them onto the roof.

Now one of the others had located the big hay barn and apparently chosen it for his own. It was Hack. Bannister, in the shadows of the haymow, watched him pull his big bay around with a yank that must have wrenched the animal's jaw, and feed it the spurs. He came straight on, unsuspecting; his bearded mouth opened on a shout, and the torch circling his head poured out its trail of stinking smoke. Bannister held his gun ready, knowing that with a .32 he must wait for his target.

Suddenly, over at the house, the Jackmans' rifles had opened fire simultaneously. One of the pair smashing full tilt into them was hit; he lost his torch and went somersaulting backward off the saddle. His horse, already terrified by the stench of burning oil and now by the sudden gunfire, careened sideward and slammed hard against the second rider, causing that one to lose control of his own mount. Bannister heard, faintly, a shout of triumph from the defenders as they saw this first attempt thrown back.

Below him, big Hack Foley had hauled rein and was twisting about in the saddle to find out what had gone wrong. In a matter of seconds, surprise had turned the tables on the Foleys and put them into a wild confusion, though one or two were settling down enough, now, to get their mounts under control and try to answer the fire that was continuing from over at the house. Hack lifted the leathers, apparently meaning to boot the gelding around and get back to help the others.

That was when Bannister stepped full into the open doorway and, cupping a palm to his mouth, called down to him: "Hack! Hack Foley! *Over here!*"

The big man heard. His head snapped around and he saw Bannister; with a bellow of rage from deep in that barrel chest he kicked the bay straight forward, the torch arcing about his head. Once, twice, and then he let go. The stick and its burning mass of oil-soaked rag came lobbing, lopsidedly end over end, and struck the opening where Jim Bannister stood.

Blinding heat seemed to envelop him momentarily. He ducked and then, through the stinking film of smoke, fired downward.

The bay chose that moment to toss its head, trying to rear, and took the bullet meant for its rider. It went crashing, carrying the man down with it. But Hack Foley was able to scramble free and, crouched above his thrashing horse with one leg still bent across the saddle, he swung a sixshooter up and fired. The bullet ate a sliver of wood from the edge of the hay door, inches from Bannister's shoulder.

Bannister shot back, aiming for the thick chest of the man below him. He didn't know if he hit or missed, this time, for suddenly he had to give attention to the blazing torch that was rolling under his feet. Flames had begun licking at the wooden floor of the loft, and half-cured hay was smoldering. He gave the torch a boot that sent it spinning out through the door, kicked burning hay after it. When he could look below again, he saw the bay lying dead and the torch sputtering itself out in the mud. But there was no sign of Hack. Apparently he had missed both shots.

Out in the yard, meanwhile, the Foleys were still getting the worst of it. A second horse was down, thrashing, and there was the sprawled shape of a man obviously either dead or at least seriously wounded. Yet they seemed unshaken in their determination to get fire onto the roof of that house, and to do it by frontal attack— apparently with no strategy at all. Again and again they were trying it, not even bothering to take cover; and the defenders kept driving them off. Meanwhile a horse with an empty saddle was running in a panic around the yard, adding to the mixup and confusion. Over at the stock pen the Jackman animals had caught the contagion and were nearly going crazy.

Bannister caught sight of one rider who had himself braced in the stirrups and was starting the windup for a long cast, the firebrand making smoky circles about the crown of his hat. It was poor range for a small-caliber hand gun but Bannister decided to try it, resting his forearm against the edge of the door to steady it and remembering not to overshoot. He touched the trigger; smoke swept across his vision. When he blinked it away he saw the man had dropped his torch and was bowed over the

saddlehorn, obviously hit. But another rider—
his mustache looked like Morgan Foley's—
pulled in close and put out a hand to settle
him, and afterward trapped the reins and
spurred away out of the fight, with the hurt
rider's mount in tow.

Now somebody else—it was Mitch Dekin—saw
the fallen torch sputtering on the ground and
rode over to lean from the saddle and scoop it
up. Bannister palmed off a quick shot, not
aiming. It must have been close enough, however, because Mitch unfolded abruptly, snatching
back his arm; and seconds later a steel shoe
gave the burning stick a glancing blow and sent it
rolling away under the hoofs of the horses.

Jim Bannister looked at his gun to see how
many bullets were left him, and in so doing he
missed the end of the fight. It was over as quick
as that. He heard no order given, saw no signal
to retreat. What had been a raid simply disinte-
grated and took off in a dying rush of hoofbeats. He was left staring down at the wreckage of
it—and at a kerosene tin lying abandoned in the
dirt, one side bashed in, its contents gurgling
out to make a black and pungent circle.

Suddenly aware of a congestion in his chest,
he drew a lungful of the chill autumn wind that
had the reek of powdersmoke and burning oil.
A weight of depression settled on him, in the
aftermath of excitement. He thought: If they'd

brought it off it would have been my fault—I gave them the excuse and the reason to think they could get away with this. . . .

Yonder at the house, the door opened now and he saw that the defenders were beginning to move cautiously into the open, as though they could scarcely believe it was safe. Bannister turned to the wooden loft ladder and started slowly down.

He had set one boot on the dirt floor of the barn and was standing like that, about to turn, arms still raised and one hand holding Tansy Jackman's revolver, when he heard the sound behind him—the unmistakable click of a gun sear. It was a chilling sound, enough to make him freeze where he was. *Hack Foley!* he thought, remembering too late that he had lost sight of the big fellow, after the exchange of shots that dropped the horse from under him.

A voice in the shadows at his back, then—the faintest whisper: "Bannister. . . ."

For an instant Jim Bannister groped toward the idea of trying to move around, trying to get in a first shot with the .32; but a cocked gun at his back made this worse than futile. Instead, holding himself otherwise completely still, he slowly turned his head. There against the open door he made out the silhouette of a shoulder, and an edge of shapeless hatbrim. The voice said, in the same breathy whisper, "Got you, you bastard!"

A painful tightness settled into Bannister's upraised arms, into his chest, into his shoulders. He knew he had to make a move—*any* move, rather than stand here and take a bullet either in the back or in the side of his turned head, whichever Foley willed.

And then, as he stood hurriedly debating, he saw the big man's silhouette change shape. Hack Foley was starting to lean sideward. There was a faint scuffing sound of his boots in the straw of the barn floor, the scrape of cloth against a roof timber. Suddenly he collapsed and fell into a heap, rolling over onto his back as his body struck the dirt. The gun spilled from his hand.

When Bannister went to stand over him, he could see the blood that drenched the man's shirtfront. He understood, then. The second of his bullets had struck Foley full in the chest. He had managed to drag himself here to cover. But, being an ox of a man, it had taken him an astonishing time to die.

Bannister shoved Tansy's little gun behind his waistband and, with a certain inward distaste, leaned to unfasten the buckle of his own gun-belt and pull it free, Hack Foley's heavy body giving ponderously. He flipped the belt into place where it belonged, around his own lean hips. After that he got his revolver from off the floor, shook a wisp of loose straw from it and looked at the loads. Two bullets had been fired.

Automatically, he punched out the empties, replacing them from the loops of the belt, and dropped the gun into its holster. It felt natural there.

About to leave, he noticed the hat that had fallen from Hack Foley's head and he stepped back for another glance at it. It looked familiar; he picked it up, and sure enough it was his own sweated-out Stetson. Trying to punch some shape into it, Bannister said aloud, "Now, why the hell would he want *that?*" He pulled the hat on and walked out and across the yard to join the knot of people in front of the house.

He might have expected jubilation; but they were subdued and silent, as though overwhelmed by what they had just gone through. Noah Jackman was hunkered down beside one of the raiders, using the man's own neck cloth to plug a bleeding shoulder wound, while Uncle El stood by holding the Spencer and watching him work. Noah lifted a white and somber face to greet Bannister. "You came through all right?" he demanded, and, as the latter nodded: "Good God! Everything happened so fast! I still can't understand it!"

Uncle El had lost some of his wispy indefiniteness. "All I know is, if we'd stood up to them Wyoming cattle barons the way we done here, we might still have the ranch they took from us."

The younger man shook his head. "It ain't an

easy thing to do—to shoot somebody and see him fall. Here's a man wounded, and Jed Foley lyin' yonder, dead. . . ."

"Hack Foley, too," Bannister said. "You'll find what's left of him in the barn. The brains, and the bully," he added. "Doesn't leave much of that outfit! The sheriff will probably run the rest of them out of the country, after this—and no loss to anyone!"

A few yards farther on, Jed Foley lay in his own blood, the upturned face looking somehow even crueler and more hawklike in death. Clay Evans lifted a fascinated stare to Bannister. "Jim! I got him! I wanted Hack, but at any rate I got one of 'em!"

"Where'd you promote the gun?" Bannister asked, indicating the snubnosed revolver in the boy's fingers. Clay lifted it, and grinned.

"Tooken it off the lawyer," he said. "Looked to me like *he* wasn't gonna use it." He turned to Claude Pine then and, deliberately reversing ends, offered the gun butt first. "Guess you can have your popgun back now, lawyer man." His swollen lips shaped an insolent grin as the plump fingers reached for it. "But I wouldn't get any ideas about using it. I'm afraid it's empty. I shot 'er dry."

Claude Pine stiffened. He looked around at the watching faces. "I see." His mouth settled into an angry line and with a grimace he snatched the useless weapon, shoved it into his pocket. "So, you win after all, Bannister!" he said harshly. "Between you and your friends, what chance has the law got?"

"We don't believe in collecting head money on friends," Noah Jackman told him. "And it looks like you're outnumbered here."

"It does!" the man agreed through tight lips. Jim Bannister stood silent, carefully not goading him, while Pine looked again at the refuse of the battle. The dead horses were already stiffening; they would have to be hauled out of the ranchyard, removed somewhere and burned. Noah Jackman had made the hurt man reasonably comfortable for the moment with his back resting against the trunk of the big cottonwood. The lawyer said stiffly, "Sheriff's going to want to see this man, and the pair that were killed. He should be notified as soon as possible. Someone tell Mrs. Harper I'm hitching the team; I'd like to leave at once."

"I'll tell her," Bannister said. He got the briefest of looks, and the lawyer walked away toward the corral. Turning to the others, Jim Bannister asked, "Where is she? And the girl?"

"In the house," Uncle El told him. "Tansy got hit during the shooting."

Jim Bannister stared. "She *what?*"

"Nothing serious," the old man explained. "Bullet just nicked her arm a little." But Bannister didn't hear him. He was already covering the distance to the house, in a few long strides; he wrenched open the door, to see Tansy Jackman seated at the kitchen table and Kate Harper just tying off a neat swath of white bandage on her forearm.

At sight of Bannister the girl cried, "Jim! You aren't hurt?" She held up the arm; she was grinning, but her face was white. "Look what happened to me. Isn't this the silliest thing? I was the only one got so much as a splinter."

"Is it bad?"

"It's nothing at all."

Kate Harper, busily preparing to put away the materials she had been using, said sternly, "You know you could have been killed!"

"Oh, I don't reckon."

But the woman stopped and looked at her directly, and her homely face was frowning and serious. "Frankly, I don't understand. I ordered you people off this ranch. When that drunken mob attacked, I'd have thought you would run and save yourselves, not stand and risk your lives to drive them off!"

The girl frowned as though she didn't quite understand. "One thing we ain't," she said, indignantly, "is quitters!"

"That seems plain," Mrs. Harper had to agree. She added, "Another thing that's plain is that I can't run this ranch myself, any more than my brother Sam could. Frankly, I like the looks of what you people did here. I wonder if you'll let me change my mind, and offer you the partnership you say my brother promised you?"

Tansy got to her feet so suddenly that her chair all but tipped over. "You really mean this? But you said—"

"I know what I said!" the woman agreed, crisply. "But I feel now it's time I stopped letting Mr. Pine do my thinking for me."

Tansy swallowed hard. She looked over at Bannister and he thought her eyes held a hint of tears. "I—I can't begin to—Oh, just wait till I tell the others!"

Footsteps at the door, then, and Bannister moved aside as Clay Evans hurried in to say, "That lawyer's pawin' the ground out there, Miz Harper. He wants to know if you're ready."

"I suppose I am." She picked up her reticule, and a shawl she had brought with her. But at the door a word from Bannister made her pause.

"Just a minute." As she turned to look at him questioningly, he jerked a head toward the boy. "What happens to him? Are you and Pine going to throw him to the sheriff? Remember, he didn't *have* to tell you it was him killed Sam Murdock! I was there that day. I saw it happen, and I'll tell you he was pushed into it. I'll take oath it's the truth!"

The woman faced him directly. "Have I said I didn't believe it?"

He hesitated. "No, you haven't. And I suppose the sheriff will listen to reason, about someone that helped bust the Foleys for him. But, what about Claude Pine?"

"I'll tell you about Mr. Pine," she answered calmly. "He has one ambition at the moment, and that's to continue handling Sam Murdock's estate. He can be made to understand that, in order to do it, there are certain things he'll have to keep his mouth shut about." She turned to the boy then. "Tell me, young man. Would you like a job?"

A look of suspicious unbelief moved across the kid's puffed and battered features, and narrowed the sharp black eyes. "A job? Would you mean—here? At Spur?"

"It's what I had in mind," she said. "Of course, it would have to be agreeable with these folks."

"I'm sure it'd be more than agreeable," Tansy said quickly. "We can use help, all right. In the worst way!"

"Well, then?" Kate Harper prodded.

When the kid still hesitated, peering at her from under lowered brows, Jim Bannister felt his patience slip. "Take the chip off your shoulder, boy!" he said gruffly. "She's all right. She wants to help you. Let her do it. Don't be so damned suspicious of everybody!"

Slowly, then, the boy nodded. "Thank you, ma'am," he grunted, barely audible. "I'd like to work for you. I'd like it fine."

Kate Harper paused a moment longer, studying the boy with an expression that somehow made her plain, old-maid's face seem almost beautiful. Some impulse—some center of starved affection—made her put out a hand and touch Clay Evans' puffed and bruised cheek. Then she turned abruptly, and young Evans followed her out and down the gallery steps where Claude Pine stood scowling beside the rented buggy, impatiently waiting to be gone.

Jim Bannister closed the door, and found himself alone with Tansy Jackman. The sound of the buggy and team reached them, starting up and quickly fading. Bannister indicated it with a movement of his head. "Soon as they reach town with the news, the sheriff will be on his way up here. It gives me a little time. I'd better use it."

He had left his coat hanging on the back of a chair. He went and got it. Remembering the .32 he had borrowed from Tansy, he took it from behind his belt and placed it on the table. Glancing around, he saw her looking at him with eyes that were too large and too bright, above a mouth that she appeared to be holding firm with an effort.

She said, in an odd voice, "This is goodbye, isn't it?"

"Yes," he said. "Yes, Tansy. I suppose it is." He shrugged into the coat, watching her.

Her lips worked on words that wouldn't come.

Suddenly she blurted, "If things do work out—if you do get squared around with the law—do you reckon you'll ever—" She fumbled again. Her cheeks took on color as she got the words spoken. "Will you marry again?"

He paused in buttoning the coat, and frowned with thought. "I've wondered about that—and I just don't know. It all seems pretty remote. Because, as far as I'm concerned—"

"It's still Marjorie?"

He nodded slowly. "You don't have the thing we had, and forget it all after a few months have passed."

"I understand. . . ." She turned her face away quickly. She walked to the window and stood with her back to him, looking out into the yard.

Jim Bannister settled the hang of the coat above his filled holster. He took his hat from the chair where he had dropped it, on entering, and walked over to her. He put a hand on her shoulder. "You're a fine girl, Tansy," he said gently, "and I know of a good man who'd marry you in a minute, if you'd only give him a chance."

For a moment he didn't think she heard. But she came about, slowly, and her frown held real puzzlement. "What did you say?" And then: "You wouldn't mean—*Noah?*"

"Does that strike you as funny? He's not really your cousin, you know."

"Well—" She hesitated. "No. Not funny, I guess. Only—" She shook her head. "I never had any idea!"

"You could do worse," Bannister said. "A lot worse."

She seemed to be considering; she seemed genuinely intrigued. "Noah Jackman! Who in the world would ever have thought—"

Her head was tilted; her lips pursed slightly, and then they took on a hint of a smile, and her eyes turned roguish. "Well," she said in a serious tone, "but he'd have to ask me! You can see that, can't you? I really couldn't be expected to marry a man unless he asked me. . . ."

Within an hour of leaving Spur, Jim Bannister caught the first sounds of a horseman at his back. Quickly alert, he picked his spot, drew his gun, and waited. Presently the cantering of a horse drifted out of the trees above him, and a rider broke into the open and came warily down the steep trail. His attention was on what his horse was doing, just then, and his hands were busy with the reins. When Bannister kneed his own horse out to confront him, Sid Parrott was taken entirely by surprise.

He pulled up so hard that his animal nearly went onto its haunches. He could only sit blinking with surprise, looking at the gun and unprotesting when Bannister moved closer and slipped the sheriff's weapon from its holster. Afterward Bannister put his own gun away.

"You were a bit quicker than I expected," Bannister said. "I figured I'd have six to ten hours, at the very least."

The lawman shrugged and put his hands on the saddlehorn. A wind that had the chill promise of fall in it swayed the pines, combed the manes of the horses, and tugged at the riders' coattails. Sid Parrott said, "Just a coincidence. I happened to remember you'd left your sorrel with the Jackmans, and I rode up this morning on the chance you might have been by to pick it up. I ran into Claude Pine and Mrs. Harper on the road; they filled me in on what happened at Spur." He wagged his head. "Them Foleys— looks like they really done themselves in this time. So there's *some* good news, at least. I'll have to go and finish them off, one of these days."

"Thought it would please you." Bannister gestured. "Get down."

His wrinkled face expressionless for once, the sheriff complied. Dismounted, he stood in the trail like a man patiently awaiting his fate. Bannister said, "That's a Jackman horse, isn't it?"

"Figured I'd need a fresh bronc, or I'd have no hopes of running you down. I switched my saddle at Spur."

The other nodded. He leaned, got the split reins of the sheriff's horse, knotted them and hung them on the saddlehorn. He moved the bronc around in the trail so that it faced uphill, the way it had come. He was saying, meanwhile, "I really hate to do this; I kind of like you, Sheriff. But you can understand I have to at least try to get myself a decent start."

The lawman said nothing. Drawing the sheriff's gun from behind his belt where he had momentarily placed it, Bannister suddenly tapped the gray sharply across the rump with its barrel. The animal bolted, shying off into a startled canter; dirt and gravel showered under its hoofs as they dug into the steep hill surface. It jingled on up the trail, finally disappearing into ridgetop timber.

Sid Parrott said reproachfully, "This is kind of tough country to be set afoot in."

"He'll head for the home corral," Bannister pointed out, "and then the Jackmans are bound to come looking to see what happened. You can start hoofing it, of course, or you can wait. Suit yourself. But you'll be all right." Deliberately he rolled out the cylinder of the gun, shook the shells into his palm and tossed them aside. He flipped the cylinder into place again, reversed ends, and handed the sheriff back his gun. The lawman eyed him coldly as he accepted it.

Reins in his hands again, Bannister lingered to stare down at the other man, dissatisfied and wishing he could somehow leave things between them on a better basis. "Sheriff," he began.

"You have what you want!" Sid Parrott cut him off, his voice hard with anger and self-disgust. "Now why don't you get the hell out of here?"

Stung, Jim Bannister straightened; he lifted the reins, with a nod. "All right, Sid. It's just that you're a good man; I've got nothing personal against you. I hope you believe that."

When he got no other answer than a silent stare, he turned the sorrel down-trail and touched it with his heel. He had thought the sheriff might make a hurried effort to reload his gun, the moment his back was turned; but when he halted at the foot of the trail, just before moving into the trees, he saw the lawman standing motionless where he had left him.

Minutes later, climbing again, he found another point where he could peer back and down through an opening in the screen of timber. Sid Parrott was still there; as Bannister watched he saw him turn, look about, and then let himself down to the ground, making his shoulders comfortable against a windfall. He seemed to be building a cigarette. He had the appearance of a man settling himself to wait.

Jim Bannister spoke to the sorrel, and rode on into the thick of the forest.

Center Point Large Print
600 Brooks Road / PO Box 1
Thorndike, ME 04986-0001 USA

(207) 568-3717

US & Canada:
1 800 929-9108
www.centerpointlargeprint.com